C000293229

THE FAMILY TRAP

LORNA DOUNAEVA

INKUBATOR
BOOKS

Published by Inkubator Books
www.inkubatorbooks.com

ISBN (eBook): 978-1-83756-045-5
ISBN (Paperback): 978-1-83756-046-2
ISBN (Hardback): 978-1-83756-047-9

PROLOGUE

Her skin prickled as she watched him rest his long legs on the mahogany coffee table. He reached down and massaged the soles of his feet. There was a slight whiff of cheese as he pulled off his socks and wriggled his long, hairy toes.

Raindrops patted the roof in a gentle rhythm, like restless fingers tapping against a bar. She sipped her own drink slowly and caressed her neck with her fingers. Her heart was drumming too now, beating along with the rain.

He took another gulp of his wine, eyes still fixed on the TV. They'd already seen this programme, but he still snickered at all the jokes as if he'd never heard them before. She wished she had the ability to blot things out like that. *Must be nice.*

He peered into his empty glass, seemingly confused as to what had happened to its contents. His eyes flickered. His head drooped a little.

"We're out of booze," she stated.

She was met with a blank stare. His eyes looked red and veiny.

"We could go to the off-licence?" she suggested.

The corners of his mouth lifted, and the rain pounded harder.

"Come on, then."

She brought him his shoes and helped him slip them on. He wobbled as he rose from the sofa. She wrapped an arm around his sweaty body and guided him through the house to the garage. It was cold and dark in there. The lights buzzed as they stumbled down the stone steps. She opened the car door for him, and he settled into the seat. She reached over to fasten his seatbelt.

"You're the best," he murmured. She climbed in the other side and started the engine, then patted her hip.

"Just need to grab my purse," she told him.

His eyes were already closing. He was nodding off the way he always did, mouth wide open, drool dribbling down his chin. She opened the car windows and stepped out, leaving the engine running. She paused to close the garage doors behind her, then retreated into the house and up to bed.

1

PRUDENCE

The young woman swept through the bar. She wore a tight-fitting T-shirt with a red hour glass emblazoned across it, like a black widow spider. Of all her features, her eyes were the most striking: large and fixed deep in their sockets. Her gaze skimmed the table laden with cards and bouquets of flowers before landing on Prudence's teenage son, Nathan.

Prudence turned her attention away from the young woman when her oldest friend, Heidi, spoke.

"So, what are you going to do with yourself now?" Heidi asked.

Prudence summoned a careless smile. "I'd like to say nothing, but I need to sort out the house and garden. Do all those little jobs I've been putting off."

She felt a rush of glee at the thought that she didn't have to set her alarm clock in the morning. Except she'd probably get up anyway to make sure Nathan was in time for uni, and then she might as well make him some toast, otherwise he wouldn't bother to eat anything. After all, breakfast was the most important meal of the day.

She glanced over at her son again. He had slipped an arm around Zoe's narrow waist.

"Oh, is that the new girlfriend?" Heidi asked. "She's pretty."

"Is she?"

Prudence scrutinised Zoe's swishy black hair and crimson lips. Nathan had been seeing her since the beginning of term, but Prudence had only met the girl briefly. They were always out, the two of them. Off to this gig or that. Zoe liked all the same bands as Nathan and apparently they both loved Thai food, so it was no wonder they'd clicked.

Heidi handed her a glass of sparkling water.

"What's this?"

"Drink it. You'll thank me in the morning."

"I'd rather have another Prosecco."

"And you will. In a bit. You need to pace yourself. You've got the whole night ahead of you."

Perhaps Heidi had a point. More friends and colleagues arrived and each insisted on buying her another drink. She now had three large glasses of wine lined up in front of her.

"Did they make a fuss of you at work?" Heidi asked.

"You wouldn't believe the speech my boss made. You'd think she'd never met me, the way she kept consulting her notes. And then she had the gall to come up to me afterwards and offer me more money to stay on."

"How much?"

"Not enough. Not by a long shot. Besides, where was the extra money when I asked for a raise back in January? They couldn't seem to find it then. And now they'll have to replace me with agency nurses who earn twice as much."

"She didn't even chip in for your leaving pressie," murmured Caroline, one of Prudence's work friends. "Still, it was true what she said. The place won't be the same without you."

Prudence laughed. "Only because no other bugger wants to be in charge."

"You've got that right."

Prudence lifted one of her wine glasses to her lips and took a long, satisfied sip. She had loved nursing, but she was done. The hospital's problems were not hers anymore. From now on, she was going to focus on the things that really mattered, like this wine and her Old English Sheepdog, Bob. And Nathan, of course.

Her gaze travelled to the dance floor. Nathan moved like he was trying to transfer a heavy urn from one shoulder to the other, while Zoe messed up her hair and wiggled her bum. *Did that count as dancing these days?*

Caroline whispered something in the DJ's ear and the music went down tempo. The dance floor emptied as people headed to the bar, but Zoe turned and buried her head in Nathan's chest. They held each other tight, barely moving, their two heads close together. Prudence could almost feel the heat coming off their bodies.

"Young love," Heidi swooned. "Aren't they cute together?"

"Hmm."

"Don't you like her?"

"I'm reserving judgement."

"Oh, they're coming over!"

Heidi gave Nathan a little wave, while Prudence rearranged her features.

"How does it feel to be officially old?" Nathan asked, giving her a quick hug.

"Cheeky!"

She reached up and fluffed his pale blond hair, then turned her attention to Zoe. "Glad you could make it."

"I've heard all about you!" Heidi interrupted. "He's besotted. It's been Zoe this and Zoe that. I was beginning to think he was making you up."

Nathan blushed. "She's exaggerating."

"I can assure you I'm not. Now, can I buy you a drink? Glass of Prosecco? Or are you more of a lager girl, Zoe?"

"Nothing for me, thanks."

"Oh, are you driving?"

"Nope."

A slow smile spread across Zoe's lips and Prudence's spine straightened. She scrutinised her son's face. His eyelashes lowered. Then Zoe fixed her with a penetrating stare.

"I'm pregnant."

The music stopped and her words filled the room.

The blood rushed to Prudence's head. "Are you sure?"

Nathan ran a hand through his hair. "We're sure."

Her eyes flitted to Zoe's abdomen. Did she look ever so slightly bloated? It was hard to say.

"I mean, you've taken a pregnancy test?"

"Three."

Prudence felt an uncomfortable tightness in her chest and throat. All the hopes and dreams she had for Nathan, his brilliant life, his brilliant career. He was too young. They were both too young. Just eighteen years old. This was a disaster.

She stood abruptly and the table trembled. Wine glasses slid off and smashed. The fragments scattered far and wide, as if propelled by an invisible hand.

"*Shit.*"

She bent to pick up the pieces, but Caroline waved her away. "I'll see to this. You deal with your family."

Prudence felt warmth in her cheeks. "I ... think I need some fresh air."

Sweat drenched her back as she burst into the pub garden. Heidi followed her outside. The wooden deck looked out over the River Soar. The water level was high today, and the river was in full fury, foamy and white.

"Mum?"

Nathan and Zoe clutched each other's hands, as they walked towards her.

She turned and leaned against the railings. "How did this ... why weren't you more careful?"

Nathan skewered her with a look. "We were careful."

"These things happen," Heidi said softly.

"How far along are you?"

"We don't exactly know," Nathan said. "Zoe's got a dating scan next week."

"Right."

She'd been to the doctor then. *How long had she known? How long had Nathan known?*

"What are you going to do?"

Zoe squared her shoulders. "I don't know. We're going to decide after the scan."

"Well, whatever you choose, it's going to be hard."

She didn't mean to sound so harsh. That was just how she felt. Whatever Zoe did, it was going to have major repercussions. Prudence couldn't imagine having a baby at eighteen. There had been so much else she'd wanted to do. Nathan hadn't come along until she was in her forties. She'd almost left it too late.

Zoe pulled her dark hair back into a ponytail. "I know this must be a shock for you. Believe me, it was a shock for me, too."

Prudence nodded. The sharp breeze had taken the heat out of her cheeks.

"What about your mum? Have you told her?"

Zoe nodded.

"What does she think?"

"She's not sure. It depends. She said it wasn't exactly what she had in mind for me."

Zoe's face crumpled, all the hardness disappearing, and for a moment Prudence thought she was going to cry.

"We'd better go back in," Heidi said, pointing towards the party. "There are a lot of people in there, all wanting to congratulate you on your retirement."

Nathan forced a smile. "Yeah, Mum, your public awaits."

It was the last thing Prudence felt like, but Heidi was right. All these people had come to see her.

She looked at Zoe. "Why don't you come back to the house after? If you're not too tired."

"I doubt I'll be able to sleep anyway," Zoe said, looking small and lost.

Prudence touched her arm. "Take it easy, okay? We'll talk more later."

The rest of the evening passed in a blur. There were drinks, toasts, and laughter, but most of it went over Prudence's head. She couldn't think about anything but the baby and everything that it would mean. Would Nathan have to give up uni? She hoped not. He wasn't a natural student. He'd had to work really hard to get there. She hated the thought of him dropping out now. She knew it took two to tango, but a part of her resented Zoe for putting him in this position, which was totally unfair of her. She knew the baby would have an even greater impact on Zoe's life. If she chose to keep it.

THE STUDENTS WERE out in force as they drove home through Loughborough town centre. She waited impatiently for a group of teenage girls to clear out of the road. If she had been driving, Prudence would have beeped the horn, but Heidi, who drove like a sloth on holidays, didn't seem bothered in the least. In the back seat, Nathan and Zoe cuddled up close, talking in soft voices. Prudence strained to listen but she couldn't make out what they said.

Heidi turned into Cherry Tree Gardens and dropped them off outside number nineteen. Prudence had left the outside lights on, illuminating the sunbeam yellow facade. She put the key in the door, and Bob the sheepdog shuffled over to greet them, taking a particular interest in their guest.

Zoe declined to pet him. She strode into the lounge without removing her shoes and headed for the large arch window. Prudence found vases for all her flowers, then sank down on the sofa. Nathan poured them both a brandy while Zoe strolled around the room as if she were trying to create a map in her mind.

"Why don't you sit down?" Prudence asked.

"I get restless legs."

Prudence took a sip of her drink and attempted to draw out Zoe's thoughts as to what she wanted to do about the baby. "Which way are you leaning at the moment?" she asked gently.

"I'm not sure," Zoe said.

"Had you ever thought about having children before this?"

"Can't say I had."

Prudence tilted her head. "Not at all?"

"Nope." She looked at Nathan. "I would like to have children ... one day."

Prudence glanced at Zoe again, but her face remained unreadable. She wasn't going to get anything out of Zoe tonight.

She finished her drink, and they all went upstairs to bed. Apparently, Zoe was spending the night in Nathan's room. Prudence wasn't sure how she felt about that, but since Zoe was already pregnant it seemed pointless to object.

. . .

IN THE MIDDLE of the night, she heard a little whine. Bob was at her door. She got up to let him in. Across the hall, she saw that Nathan's door was wide open. He appeared to be alone in the bed. Where was Zoe? Prudence should have left it, but instinct had her padding down the hall to the bathroom. It was empty. Bob at her heels, she walked out onto the landing and peered down into the lounge below. Zoe stood at the little bureau, going through the drawers.

"Zoe?"

Zoe jumped abruptly, but she didn't attempt to hide what she was doing.

"Prudence! Hi! I was ... do you have any headache tablets? My head is pounding."

"I keep the medicine in the kitchen," she said pointedly, and walked through to her well-stocked medicine cabinet. She took down a packet and handed it to Zoe. "Here, these won't harm the baby."

"Thank you."

Zoe's fingers were cold as they brushed against hers. Prudence poured her a glass of water and watched while she took the pills. She thought Zoe would go back up to Nathan's room, but instead she returned to the sofa.

"You really should try to sleep."

Zoe met her eyes. "I'll try in a bit."

"Well, night then."

"Night."

Prudence put one foot on the stairs then turned, nearly tripping over Bob. "Look, I'm sorry if I overreacted a little earlier. It was a shock. I promise you, it will be all right, love. Whatever you decide."

"Thank you."

Zoe's mouth curved into a smile that didn't quite reach her eyes.

2

PRUDENCE

Prudence lay back down, with Bob snuggled up beside her. He usually slept on the end of Nathan's bed, but she didn't have the heart to send him away. She closed her eyes and tried to drift back to sleep, but adrenaline coursed through her veins. She couldn't believe she was going to be a grandma. It was a lot to take in.

She tried to picture her sweet, slightly awkward son as a father. It wasn't so long ago he was tripping over his shoelaces and playing Dungeons & Dragons with his friends. Zoe looked young too, despite her trendy make-up and fashionable attire. They were both little more than kids, really. What a shame this couldn't have happened a few years down the road, by which time they'd know if they were right for each other.

It occurred to her that she knew very little about Zoe, apart from what Nathan had told her. She sat up in bed and pulled her laptop from its charger. Zoe had an unusual last name so she shouldn't be hard to find. She typed in 'Zoe Nithercott', but no profile came up. Maybe Twitter. No. LinkedIn? Instagram? Nothing. This was strange. She'd thought everyone under the age of thirty was hooked on social media. The girl had to have some kind of digital footprint. A mention in a local newspaper? Something. But no, no Zoe Nithercott came up at all.

She closed the laptop and set it down, but her mind was still buzzing. *That girl, trapping her son.*

She gave herself a shake. *She probably doesn't know what's hit her.*

She heard Zoe coming up the stairs, and there was a little click as she went into Nathan's room and shut the door behind her. Perhaps she's on Pinterest, Prudence thought, reaching for her laptop again, but there was no Zoe Nithercott to be found there either. Prudence gave up. She was never going to sleep now. She might as well watch TV. She grabbed the remote and watched one true crime documentary after another. She had always had a morbid fascination with these shows. There was something intriguing about the lengths murderers went to. Whilst she was horrified at each of the atrocities they committed, a part of her always wondered whether some of the victims couldn't have been a little less gullible. They never seemed to expect anything bad to happen to them, not until it was far too late.

A WEEK LATER, Prudence sat in the waiting room, surrounded by pregnant women. One of them was stroking her stomach, as if to emphasise the fact that she was pregnant, while her partner brought her a drink of water.

Prudence glanced nervously at the clock and tried to focus on her gardening magazine, but the article on terracotta hanging baskets held no interest. She wished she'd gone in there with them. What if Zoe had it all wrong? What if she wasn't pregnant at all? Or worse still, what if there was something wrong with the baby? She didn't want her son's girlfriend to be pregnant, but nor did she want the decision taken out of their hands.

The door opened.

"Mum?"

Nathan's cheeks were flushed. Zoe looked pale.

Prudence hurried over to them. "How did it go?"

"I'm fifteen weeks gone," Zoe said faintly.

For a moment, Prudence thought she'd heard her wrong. "Fifteen weeks?" *How was that possible?* "Are you sure? You don't even look ..."

Nathan held out a picture and she looked at it. A dark blob with a huge head. It looked pretty much the same as any scan picture except this was her son's baby. Her grandchild. She couldn't stop staring at it. Up until now the baby had just been an abstract idea, but this was real. A little life.

"So what are you going to do?"

"I think I want to be a dad," Nathan said. They both looked at Zoe.

"I think I want that too."

Nathan gripped Zoe's hand tighter. Prudence felt him exhale.

"Well, then. I suppose I'm going to be a grandmother."

She took another look at the picture and felt a twinge of excitement. "Shall we get a coffee?" she suggested, as they walked down the corridor. She already missed her regular lattes at the coffee shop.

"You go ahead," Zoe said. "I'm going to ring my mum."

NATHAN AND PRUDENCE walked towards the hospital coffee shop. "What else did they say? Is everything growing normally? Is the head the right size?"

"Yes, Mum, it's all completely fine."

They joined the queue and Nathan browsed the selection.

He could never just have a cup of coffee. Even as a baby, he'd always been permanently hungry. She didn't know where he put it.

"Thought you'd retired?" the woman at the counter said.

Prudence smiled. "It appears I'm going to be a grandmother."

"Congratulations. How exciting!"

She looked at Nathan, who mumbled something incoherent. She wondered if he was embarrassed, but he would have to get used to the attention. She paid for their lattes, plus a hot sandwich for Nathan. Then they found themselves a table.

"Give me another look at the picture," she said. He handed it over and she gazed at it, trying to make out the baby's features.

"I can't believe Zoe's so far along."

"It must have happened right at the beginning of term," he said. "She didn't have any symptoms. She hasn't been sick or anything."

"It happens," Prudence said. But she couldn't help wondering if Zoe had known. There was something rather secretive about that young lady. Perhaps she'd been weighing up her options, deciding whether Nathan would step up – after all, it was very early in their relationship. Some young men would have done a runner. She recalled how Nathan's dad had been horrified to discover he was going to be a father. Not that she'd needed anything from him. She and Nathan had been just fine on their own.

"So what happens next?"

"We have to come back in a month or so for another scan."

Nathan tore into his sandwich, devouring it as if he hadn't eaten in days, when Prudence had in fact seen him eat a bowl of cereal just an hour or so ago.

Zoe was carrying a lot of tension in her shoulders when she returned.

"What did your mum say?" Nathan asked.

Zoe looked stricken. "She's ... coming to get me at the weekend. She thinks I should leave uni and go back home."

Prudence's stomach turned over. "And where is home, Zoe?"

"Cheshire."

That was almost a two-hour drive. Nathan shot her a look, but what could she do?

"I'll come up and see you every weekend," he said.

"Or we could come down to see you." Zoe consulted her phone. "It's two and half hours by train."

"That's a long way with a baby," Prudence said.

The drive home was silent, each of them lost in their own thoughts. When Prudence dropped Zoe off at her halls of residence, all the other students were heading over to the canteen for dinner. They looked so happy and carefree. Zoe walked reluctantly behind them. She stood alone at the back of the queue, not talking to anyone. Prudence's heart ached for her.

"Mum, I don't want Zoe to go back to Cheshire," Nathan said as they drove off.

"I know, love, nor do I." She drew a deep breath. "What if we invite Zoe to move in with us? We could turn the guest room into a nursery."

Nathan's eyes lit up. "Yes! Let's do it."

"We still need to convince Zoe and her mum," Prudence said. "She might be happier going home. We have to respect her decision. It's not going to be easy for her, either way."

Nathan clasped his hands in his lap. "I really don't want to lose them—Zoe or the baby. We're a family now. We should be together."

"It's going to be hard," she warned. "Being a parent is

relentless, twenty-four hours a day. The baby will wake in the night and demand to be fed. Sometimes you'll feed it and it still won't sleep, or it will wake up again an hour later. You'll be tired and grumpy and it's going to cost a lot of money. There will be nappies, food, clothes, medicine."

"I know."

"So here's what we'll do. We'll invite Zoe and her mum round to our house. We'll get to know each other a bit and we'll make the offer. But ultimately, it needs to be Zoe's choice, okay?"

"Okay. Thanks, Mum."

PRUDENCE SPENT the rest of the week preparing. She didn't know why, but it seemed vital that the house look its best. She got out the steam cleaner and did the carpets. She even washed and ironed the curtains in the lounge. She lit pleasant-smelling candles and stocked the fridge with deli foods and snacky bits. She wanted Zoe's mum to get the right impression of them, to know that with her help Zoe and the baby would be in safe hands.

On Saturday, Zoe turned up ten minutes before her mum was expected. Prudence felt unreasonably nervous and she kept going to the window to look out. Bob bounced around at her feet, not understanding what all the fuss was about. Zoe and Nathan had both gone rather quiet and they kept sending each other long, meaningful looks, as if they were communicating telepathically. Then Prudence heard the purr of an engine outside and Zoe jumped up in excitement. She rushed to the window and Bob bounded after her.

"She's here!"

Zoe's mum drove a bright pink sports car. Prudence didn't recognise the make, and watched as she climbed out. She wore a classic white blouse, her long legs encased in tan trousers and snakeskin boots. She looked at least ten years younger than Prudence, but then most of the other mothers were. Prudence let her ring the bell. She needed a moment to compose herself before she opened the door.

"You must be Prudence. I'm Alana."

She smelled nice, like apples and honey blossom. Prudence wasn't sure if they should hug or shake hands, but Alana solved this problem by thrusting a bottle of wine into her arms.

"Oh, thank you! Just what we need."

"I'll say."

Prudence led her into the kitchen, where she dug out two glasses while Alana popped the cork.

It looked like a good bottle. The label had embossed writing and there was a little dust on the bottom, suggesting it had been dug out of a wine cellar.

They clinked glasses and she took an appreciative sip.

"I have to tell you this isn't what I wanted for my daughter. I feel like I've failed her ..." Alana spoke too fast. Her eyes shone with tears. The hand holding the wine glass shook just a little, sending a stream of liquid running down her hand and onto the counter. She rubbed it absentmindedly with the sleeve of her shirt.

"Oh, no, you can't think like that. It isn't what I wanted either, but it's happened. We need to make the most of it."

Alana nodded. "You're right, of course. It's just a little hard to accept. I don't understand why she didn't say something sooner."

"I think she was probably in denial."

"She's not the only one."

She let out a sob and wiped her eyes with the same sleeve she'd used to clean up the wine. "Oh, look at me, blubbing all over you. What must you think of me?"

"It's okay," Prudence said. "If anyone understands, it's me."

She led Alana through to the lounge. Nathan and Zoe had made themselves scarce. She heard a thump and concluded that they must have disappeared upstairs to the bedroom. Perhaps Nathan wanted her to plead their case with Alana before they came down, but Prudence didn't feel ready to do that. She had only just met the woman. It didn't seem fair.

They sat in Prudence's unusually clean lounge, devoid of all dog hairs and dust. Alana had kicked her boots off at the door and Prudence admired her glossy red toenails. She herself almost never bothered with nail varnish.

Bob poked his head in, and Alana's face broke into a smile.

"Hey! You've got a Dulux dog." Alana reached out to stroke Bob, who settled at her feet.

The wine glasses were empty already and Alana leaned over to top them both up. "You must think I'm a terrible alcky, but it simply doesn't affect me. I could drink the whole bottle and still be absolutely fine."

"Lucky you. I wish I could say the same."

Eventually, there was a creak on the stairs, and Zoe and Nathan appeared in the doorway. Prudence beckoned them inside. They were sneaking around like school children, not older teenagers on the verge of becoming parents.

"It's nice to meet you," Nathan stammered, when Alana shook his hand. The poor boy looked like he was at a job interview, Prudence thought. He kept fastening and unfastening the top button of his shirt, and damp sweaty patches were visible under both arms.

"They make a sweet couple," Alana murmured, when Nathan and Zoe went out to the kitchen to fetch the food. "Your son seems like a very mature young man."

"He is."

"Zoe said he was studying engineering. He must be bright, too."

Prudence nodded proudly. "Don't know where he gets it from."

"Oh, don't be modest. We both know that behind every great man is usually a great woman."

"Very true. Alana, if you don't mind me asking, is it just the two of you?"

"Zoe's dad is not in our lives."

"No? Nor is Nathan's. He left when Nathan was very little. But don't worry, Nathan takes after me. He is very responsible for his age."

Alana nodded. "I can see you're a strong single woman like me. So, is Nathan sure about all this?"

"He is. He really wants this baby. He wants them to be a family."

Alana smiled sadly. "I suppose it's very romantic. Just a shame they're both so young. Do you think they'll be able to cope?"

"They have us," Prudence said. *Should she ask Alana now?* She didn't want to step on the other woman's toes.

Nathan walked back in with the trays of food she'd bought from Tesco. He and Zoe laid it all out on the table. Alana reached for the wine bottle and topped them both up again. Prudence relaxed. She was enjoying this. Alana was good company.

She reached for a piece of cheese and popped it into her mouth.

Nathan kept sending her pointed looks but she ignored him. She would ask Alana when it felt right.

"Have you seen the garden?" Zoe asked, leaping to her feet.

Alana shot her a look. "Careful! Remember you have a precious life growing inside you."

"I know."

Zoe led them all outside. Prudence was a little bemused as Zoe pointed out the best features of the garden. She wasn't aware Zoe had even noticed the water feature or the rockery.

"It's not overlooked at all, is it?" Alana said. "Nice high hedges all the way round. I like that. It gives you plenty of privacy."

"Have you seen the rest of the house?" Zoe said. "You should see the wide storage shelves in the utility room."

Prudence glanced at her oddly.

"Alana is an estate agent," Nathan told her. "She loves to see people's houses."

Alana clapped her hands to her mouth. "Oh god, you must think I'm incredibly nosey!"

"No, no, it's fine," Prudence said. "Come on, I'll give you a tour."

She was proud of her house. She had put a lot of work into remodelling the kitchen and dining room into one open space with an island. And she had personally redecorated the bathroom, swapping the sickly pink tiles for more tasteful aqua and grey.

Alana seemed impressed. "I must say, I love what you've done with the place. You clearly have great taste, Prudence."

"It's surprisingly roomy, isn't it?" Zoe said. She sounded almost as if it were her own house that was being complimented.

Prudence cleared her throat. "I know you came here to bring Zoe home, but I want to offer an alternative if I may. Zoe would be most welcome to stay with us. That way she could continue her education and I'd be on hand to help with the baby when it comes. I don't know if Zoe's mentioned but

I've just taken early retirement, so I'd have plenty of time to help."

She watched as Alana digested her offer. She hoped she hadn't overstepped the mark. Zoe was Alana's daughter, after all.

"What do you think?" Alana said, looking directly at Zoe.

Zoe seemed lost for words. She looked hopelessly at Nathan.

"Zoe wants to stay," he said. "For now, at least. I've got a part-time job and we're saving to get a flat of our own. I know we'll earn better money in the long run if we both finish uni."

Zoe nodded vigorously to show that she agreed.

"And you're sure you don't mind, Prudence?" Alana asked. "You really want to take all this on? I mean, shouldn't you be off travelling the world or something?"

Prudence nodded emphatically. "I've done my share of travelling, believe me. Now I want to help Nathan and Zoe and give the baby the start he or she deserves."

"Well, then," Alana said as she reached for the bottle again. It was almost empty. Nathan rushed out to the kitchen and returned with a fresh bottle. He topped them up, then he and Zoe lay back against the sofa. They both looked relieved, now it was decided. Prudence felt good about the decision too.

"If I may, I'd like to make a toast." Alana raised her glass. "Zoe, Nathan, life has taken us in a direction I never expected, but I'm sure I speak for Prudence too when I say how proud I am of the pair of you. I know you're both going to make wonderful parents."

"I'll drink to that," Prudence said.

She couldn't help but wonder what the baby would look like. Would he or she inherit Zoe's deep-set eyes and distinctive chin? Or would it resemble Nathan, with his softer face and pale blond hair?

"Tell me, what was Nathan like when he was young?" Alana asked. "He seems a very polite, considerate boy."

Prudence laughed. "Oh, we had our moments, but he's always been easy. I'd like to say it's down to my parenting, but honestly, I think you just get the child you get. When I think of some of the crap my friends have been through with their kids, skipping school and taking drugs. Well, Nathan never put me through any of that."

Alana nodded. "I know what you mean. Zoe's a good girl but she gave me a few grey hairs when she was younger."

Prudence glanced over at Zoe and saw her shrink down into the cushions. Alana didn't seem to notice.

"From the age of about fourteen, she was out with a different boy every night, weren't you, love? Right up until she started uni."

Zoe flashed her a look, but Alana didn't seem to notice. "She's always been popular, always had her pick of the boys, but it's so nice to see her settled. Nathan is clearly a very special young man." She glanced appreciatively at Nathan, who returned to the table, hoovering up the remains of the food.

"There was this one boy, he was the captain of the football team. She snuck out with him one night. I had no idea. I thought she was fast asleep in bed, so I locked the back door and then Zoe must have come home and found both the doors locked. Now, instead of cutting her losses and ringing the bell, do you know what my crazy daughter did? She set off the fire alarm on the building next to ours and the entire neighbourhood emptied out into the street.

"Then the fire brigade arrived, but obviously there was no fire, so eventually we got the all-clear and everyone returned to their houses, dazed and confused. Zoe followed me back in and acted all innocent, like she'd had nothing to do with the whole thing, but I was on to her. Do you know why?"

Alana glanced at Zoe, but she didn't say anything. "Because I'm a mum. So of course the first thing I did when I heard that alarm was to go and wake Zoe. So I knew she wasn't there. I knew she had snuck out."

Zoe gave an odd little snort of laughter, but Prudence didn't find it funny. She was appalled that Zoe had done something so irresponsible.

"I told Zoe she was grounded and that I didn't want her seeing that boy again, but Zoe didn't care because a few days later she'd hooked up with a different boy from her science club. I liked that one better. He made her study. No more calling out the fire brigade after that."

Prudence forced a smile, but she had an uneasy feeling in the pit of her stomach. She glanced over at Nathan and saw that his mouth had become a thin line. Was he jealous, she wondered? He himself had only been out with a couple of girls before Zoe and neither of those relationships had lasted beyond a few weeks.

She studied Zoe, who appeared to be enjoying herself immensely. How could she laugh at that—didn't she have any shame? Not that a woman should be ashamed for going out with lots of men but ... A thought stabbed at her heart. When had Zoe stopped seeing those other boys? Men? Whatever they were? What if Nathan wasn't the father of her baby?

"One for the road?" Alana held up the wine bottle again.

"I think I've probably had enough," Prudence said.

"One more won't hurt. Go on, or I'll have to finish the bottle myself."

Prudence didn't have the heart to point out that nobody had to finish the bottle. Besides, it was fizzy wine. It wouldn't be any good in the morning, so she allowed Alana to top her up one last time.

"Will you be alright?" she asked, as Alana pulled on her boots.

"I'm fine. I booked myself into the hotel on the corner."

Nathan rose from his chair. "I'll walk you, if you like?"

Alana pressed a hand to her heart. "Oh, what a gentleman! But I'll be fine, thank you."

Prudence walked her guest to the door and waved her off. The house was silent now. Nathan had turned off the music, and he and Zoe had retreated up to their room, leaving behind all the mess. Prudence picked up the plates and glasses and carried them through to the kitchen. She rinsed everything and slid the plates into the dishwasher. Bob lumbered wearily against her as she went about her nightly routine, checking both doors were locked and placing the keys in the bowl where she would find them in the morning. She was about to head upstairs when she heard a strange sound. She stopped and listened. It sounded like Zoe was crying. She guessed they must be talking about what Alana had revealed. Had Nathan known Zoe had such a colourful past? He certainly hadn't mentioned it. They were talking in muffled, whispered voices, so she could not make out what was being said.

By the time she crept upstairs, past Nathan's door, the light was still on but she couldn't hear anything. She pictured Zoe sitting on the bed with her arms crossed tightly over her body, Nathan pacing the room, his long legs cramped for space because Zoe had brought her bags with her, even before everything was decided. Was he going to share the bed with her, or would he sleep downstairs on the sofa?

She yawned widely. Whatever was going on, she had to leave it to them to sort out. She retreated to her own room and promptly fell asleep. She slept soundly until she was awoken by the hum of Nathan's shaver in the bathroom. He'd got himself up then. Usually, she had to go in two or three times before she could unearth him from his bed. She dressed in her gym clothes and went downstairs to find Zoe ironing one of Nathan's shirts in the lounge.

"Morning," she said in surprise.

Zoe smiled at her brightly. "Morning. I hope we didn't wake you? Nathan's got the kettle on if you want some tea."

Nathan came in, bare chested.

"Thanks babe," he whispered into Zoe's hair. He picked up the shirt she'd just ironed and wriggled into it, pausing to kiss the nape of her neck before he did up the buttons. Prudence watched with concern. Clearly, they'd made up from yesterday's argument, but she was still no closer to knowing the answer to the great question: *Was Nathan really the father of Zoe's baby?*

3

ZOE

From: Zoe Nithercott <Zoe.Nithercott@lbro.ac.uk>
To: Ted Nithercott <Edward.Nithercott@gmail.com>
Subject: Hello

Dad,

Sorry I haven't been in touch for a while. There's been a lot going on in my life. Guess what? I've started uni. First one in our family, Mum says. I'm studying Banking and Finance, but I really want to know about cryptocurrencies because they are the future! Once I've finished with this course I'll get a job working for a new start-up because that's where all the money is.

Dad, I really like uni. Not just because I get to study my favourite subject, but because I feel like I've finally joined the world of the living. You're going to tell me to stop being so melodramatic but that's how I feel. I went to the fresher's fair on my first day and there was a club for EVERYTHING! You like playing radio DJ? There's a club for that. Medieval re-enactments? Club for that. Playing darts in the pub? Club for that. I joined the music society. That's where I met Nathan. We had an instant connection. He's got white-blond hair like Justin Bieber but don't tell him that because he hates cheesy pop. He's into Muse and Paramore. I've been to more gigs in the last few weeks than I have in my entire life.

Nathan lives with his mum, Prudence, which seemed a bit lame at first but that means he's saving loads, which makes total sense. I mean why shell out hundreds on a flat share when you can be saving for the future? I like Nathan's house. It's got a large east-facing garden and the kitchen's even bigger than ours, which is just as well because Nathan's mum is into baking. She makes cupcakes and scones and stuff. Her dinners are pretty good too, if you don't mind the vegetables. She has way too many ornaments, but all in all their house is homey. I quite like spending time there, which is just as well because they've invited me to move in with them. You might think this is a bit sudden, but Nathan and I have been seeing each other for weeks now and you might want to sit down for this, but it turns out I'm pregnant!

I know this must be a shock and I hope you're okay with it. Mum is, sort of. Now she's got used to the idea.

I think Nathan could be a good dad. He has all the right qual-ities: he's kind, responsible and very hardworking. He'll have to brush up on his dad jokes but maybe you can help him with that? He's already passed his driving test and he's got excellent taste in music so he won't embarrass the poor kid by blaring out Tom Jones songs.

I haven't made up my mind about Prudence yet. She's old and kind of frumpy and I know she is only letting me live under her roof because she wants access to the baby but I'm good with that. Like I said, it's a nice house. The old prune must have spent loads doing it up because it looks totally modern on the inside and you could easily believe it was a new build, even though Nathan has lived there all his life. So anyway, I think this could be good for me, if things go the way I want. I am happy but totally stressed about the future. I think we both know that the baby can only be one gender or this won't end well.

Zoe xxx

4

PRUDENCE

I t rained for most of Saturday morning and Prudence didn't hear a peep out of Nathan and Zoe until lunchtime, when Nathan came downstairs to make a fry-up.

"Are we okay for money, Mum?" he asked as he pulled bacon and sausages out of the fridge.

Prudence considered. "Well, I have my private pension and you have your job at Morrisons. We ought to muddle through okay."

"But will it be enough? Zoe says we need to be saving up, not just treading water."

She raised an eyebrow. "You could start by cutting back on all the gigs you've been going to. Those tickets don't come cheap."

"I know." He looked a little sad as he took out a frying pan and heated it on the hob. "I was thinking maybe I should sell my comic book collection. Some of the older ones are worth a bit."

"Oh, but you always loved your comics!"

"I love Zoe and the baby more."

She watched him crack an egg into the pan. He was growing up so fast it was almost painful to watch. She wanted to wrap him up in a blanket, the way she had when he was tiny. It had all been so much easier back then. She liked the man her son was becoming. Loved that he was willing to do anything for his family, but Alana's words still burned in her ears.

"Nathan, are you sure the baby is yours? Alana mentioned Zoe had been seeing other boys before you and she wasn't certain about the dates ..."

Nathan whirled round, eyes blazing.

"The baby is definitely mine. One hundred per cent."

"How can you be so—"

His voice dropped to a growl. "I just know."

Prudence held up her hands. "As long as you're sure."

"Mum, I'm sure."

She backed out of the kitchen. She was glad that Nathan was so sure of himself, but she couldn't get rid of her niggling doubt. There was something about Zoe that bothered her. She couldn't quite put her finger on it.

LATER, she drove into Nottingham to have a look around the shops. She'd intended to buy some new gardening trousers, but she found herself drifting over to the window of a little boutique that specialised in baby clothes. It was probably too soon to be buying anything, but she couldn't resist a look. She admired a tiny Babygro with fluffy chicks on the front, and another featuring a little sleepy bear. Before she could stop herself, she was inside the shop, watching as the cashier wrapped them in tissue paper.

"Would you like a bag?"

"No, I think I can fit it all into my handbag."

That way Zoe and Nathan wouldn't know. As far as she knew, they hadn't bought anything for the baby yet. They were still being cautious, waiting for the second scan. She felt a little guilty now about what she'd said to Nathan. Perhaps she shouldn't have said anything at all. He had seemed so adamant.

She walked out of the shop, the parcel nestled in her handbag. She had forgotten how adorable baby clothes could be and what a pleasure it was to buy them. A display in another shop window caught her eye. There were little baby hoodies and joggers in different colours of the rainbow. Such darling little things. The tissue paper rustled as she crossed the street. She would just have a quick look.

Cooking smells greeted Prudence when she arrived home. She walked through to the kitchen and found Nathan wearing her best apron. He and Zoe were giggling and teasing each other with a wooden spoon.

"Something smells good," she said.

Nathan gave her an easy grin, while Zoe dabbed furiously at the flour on her nose.

"What have you been buying?" Nathan asked.

"Oh, nothing much."

Prudence clutched her bag tightly, embarrassed by its contents. "What are you cooking?"

He finished rolling out the pastry. "Beef Wellington, we hope."

Prudence raised her eyebrows. "Right, well I'll let you get on."

She trotted upstairs to her bedroom and spread the baby clothes out on her bed. Such beautiful, delicate little things.

She put them away in the bottom of her wardrobe and looked around the room.

In her previous life, she had always been doing something. Running round the house with the hoover or cleaning the bathrooms. But she didn't feel the need now. She could just chill out if she wanted to. She had all day tomorrow to do the cleaning. She felt quite naughty, climbing into bed and pulling the covers up over her head.

A little while later, she opened her eyes to find Nathan peering in.

"What's wrong, Mum. Are you ill?"

"Not at all," she said with a grin.

"Right, well, dinner's ready. Can you open the wine?"

Zoe had set the table with the best cloth, and the house was filled with the scent of the Beef Wellington. They'd even lit some candles and dimmed the lights to give the place a bit of atmosphere.

Bob sniffed the air, eager to get his share. When he was a younger dog, he would have been right under her feet, reminding her of his presence, but these days he seemed content to just breathe in the good smells, grateful for any titbit that might come his way.

The Wellington was surprisingly good, if a little burnt around the edges, and the mashed potatoes were soft and buttery, just the way Prudence liked them.

"More wine?" Zoe asked when Prudence had drained her glass. Before she could answer, Zoe was topping her up again. Prudence smiled and leaned back. This was turning out to be a pleasant evening.

Zoe told anecdotes from her childhood. In each one, her mum did something hilarious. Prudence rattled her brain for something equally funny or outrageous, but she and Nathan had lived a quiet, sedentary existence by comparison.

"Why did you choose to study finance?" she asked Zoe.

"Money is the key to everything and cryptocurrencies are the money of the future."

"Aren't they just fake money, though? I mean, from my admittedly limited understanding, the whole cryptocurrency system is just like an elaborate house of cards."

"A pyramid scheme," Nathan supplied.

Zoe leaned forward, eyes gleaming. "Yes, that is one interpretation, but even a pyramid scheme makes money for the ones at the top, and I intend to be at the top."

The alarm on Nathan's phone sounded and he jumped up. "That'll be the apple crumble."

Zoe smiled wistfully. What was she thinking about, Prudence wondered. The baby? Or some imagined future where she would be rolling in it?

Zoe's eyes flicked back to her. "Finance is the most important subject to study," she declared. "Because it's vital for a woman to have her own money in order to be independent from men."

Prudence nodded slowly. Yes, as a single woman, she could see Zoe's point.

On Monday morning, Prudence woke naturally, and lay in bed a while, resisting the urge to be productive. Nathan had Zoe now, and she was sure that Zoe's bladder would get them both up, whether she'd set her alarm or not. She'd been up two or three times a night when she was pregnant.

Sometime later, a shaft of light burned through her retinas. She blinked into the light.

Her bedroom door was wide open and Zoe stood yawning outside the bathroom.

"Don't forget your lunchbox," she called out to Nathan. "I've packed you enough sandwiches to keep you going."

Prudence smiled. It sounded as though Zoe had it all

under control. She heard Nathan thunder down the stairs and out the door. There was a slight creaking sound from out in the hallway. She opened her eyes again. Zoe was watching her through the open door.

"Morning," Prudence called out.

"Morning."

"Don't you have any lectures this morning?"

"Yes, but I'm not going to go." Zoe yawned widely.

Prudence sat up. "What's wrong? Didn't you sleep well?"

"No. The dog was scratching at the floorboards all night. Nathan slept through it but I just couldn't."

"Sorry to hear that. He's used to sleeping on Nathan's bed, so I suppose it might take him a little while to get used to the new arrangement."

Zoe nodded wearily.

"I tell you what, I'll take him out for a walk now, and you can go back to bed for a bit."

"Thanks."

Zoe retreated into Nathan's room and closed the door behind her.

PRUDENCE PUT Bob in the car and drove to her favourite dog-walking place on the outskirts of town. The park was an old ridge and furrow meadow with gentle slopes that made the walk interesting for both her and Bob, and there was always a good choice of sticks for Bob to choose from.

The car park was quite busy that morning, but then Prudence would usually be at work at this time. She smiled as she let Bob off his lead, and he romped up and down the gentle inclines. There were no other dogs nearby to worry about, except one little scrap who walked up to Bob and yapped in his face. He stared at the young upstart, then trotted back to Prudence and stood meekly behind her.

Prudence chuckled. "Are you kidding me? A big old dog like you, scared of that little guy?"

The dog's owner stepped forward. "I do apologise. Sniffy is a terror."

Sniffy gave a loud yap that belied his small size.

"Small dog syndrome," his owner muttered.

Bob looked at Prudence with uncertainty.

"Bob, it's fine," she said in a calm voice. "He's not going to hurt you."

"He might give you a good sniff, though," his owner said. He looked directly at Prudence. "Haven't seen you here before."

She shook her head. "I normally come later, after work."

"Oh. What do you do?"

"I was a nurse. I just took early retirement." She was keen to emphasise the 'early'.

His face lit up. He had a nice smile: it started at one ear and stretched all the way across his face to the other.

"At least your job was useful. I'm a pork scratching spotter."

"What's that?"

"I'm the bloke who ensures there are no hairy bits in your pork scratchings." He wiggled his eyebrows comically and she burst out laughing. She couldn't tell if he was serious or not.

Bob wandered off and Prudence realised she'd better go after him.

"I'll let you get on. Nice talking to you," the man said.

"You, too!" Prudence called out. Bob was already halfway into the hedge.

She and Bob continued their walk until he got tired, and she had to nudge him back to the car with the promise of a treat. He just didn't have the stamina these days. He snored loudly on the journey home, and when she pulled up outside the house he pretended he wasn't up to the short walk up the path, so she had to pick him up and carry him over her shoulder like a giant rug.

She made herself a cup of tea and ate a pastry, then headed out to the garden, where she remained for most of the day. Hours melted away as she tended to the flower beds. It was so wonderful to spend the day outside, with nothing more to worry about than what to have for dinner. Nathan was going straight from uni to his shift at Morrisons that afternoon, so she knew it would just be her and Zoe eating. She opened the fridge and found all the ingredients for spaghetti bolognese. She had perfected the recipe over the years. The secret was to let the sauce simmer for at least an hour.

Zoe didn't answer when Prudence called her to the table, so she traipsed up the stairs to get her. There was no light coming from Nathan's room. Perhaps she was asleep.

"Zoe?"

She opened the door gently. Zoe sat at Nathan's desk, using the computer. She had headphones in her ears, which accounted for the fact she hadn't heard her.

"Zoe? Dinner's ready!"

Zoe slammed the laptop shut and jumped to her feet.

"Sorry! Didn't mean to startle you."

"That's alright."

Zoe grabbed her phone from the desk and followed Prudence downstairs.

"I thought we'd eat in the kitchen, since it's just the two of us," Prudence said.

Zoe shot a look at Bob, who had his head in his bowl in the corner.

Prudence sank into her chair and picked up her fork. The bolognese smelled delicious. When she looked up, Zoe was texting on her phone, her plate untouched.

"Aren't you hungry?"

Zoe spooled some spaghetti onto her fork and sucked it down like she was swallowing a forkful of wriggling worms.

Prudence turned her attention back to her own plate. It really was delicious.

"How are you feeling?" Prudence asked gently. "I remember being dog tired when I was expecting Nathan."

Zoe shrugged. "I'm okay."

"Any cravings?"

"No."

"I once licked the corner of a snooker cue. It must have been the chalk I was craving."

"Really?"

But there was no real interest in Zoe's voice. Prudence had thought that little nugget would get more response, but Zoe seemed unwilling to enter into conversation.

Zoe was texting again, her fingers moving at the speed of light. How did she do that? Prudence owned a mobile phone, but she mainly used it when she went out. When she was home, she preferred to speak to people on the landline. Her thumbs turned to plums the moment she tried to text. And she hated all those trendy abbreviations. Why couldn't people just say what they meant?

As if to prove her point, the landline began to ring. Prudence didn't normally answer the phone during dinner, but she decided to break her rule this once. It was Heidi.

"You okay? You sound funny."

"I'm fine." She could hardly say anything with Zoe sitting across the table from her.

"What are you doing tomorrow?"

"I'm swimming in the morning. Then I have to finish getting everything ready for the coffee morning. You are still coming, aren't you?"

"Wouldn't miss it. I'm baking cherry muffins."

"Yum!"

"Okay. See you at Zumba?"

"If I have time."

"Christ almighty. You're supposed to be retired."

"I know!"

Whilst Prudence had been on the phone, Zoe had slipped back upstairs, leaving her dirty plate on the table. Prudence felt a twinge of annoyance. Still, it was nothing Nathan wouldn't have done. If she expected Zoe to wash up, she probably needed to tell her so. But the prospect of going after her was so unappealing that she picked up both their plates and carried them into the kitchen herself. She had just got the dishwasher running when she heard Nathan's key in the door.

Zoe rushed downstairs, and she and Nathan fell on each other like they'd been separated for years. Prudence averted her gaze as their kisses grew longer. She turned her attention to Bob and began grooming his unkempt fur. A moment later, Zoe waltzed into the kitchen and dished up a plate of bolognese for Nathan. Prudence watched as she popped it in the microwave.

Nathan sat down at the table while Zoe fetched him a cold beer. The microwave pinged and Zoe pulled the plate out.

"Hmm, something smells good." Nathan sniffed appreciatively.

Zoe smiled and set the food in front of him. Prudence felt her stomach clench slightly as she watched Zoe fuss around her son. She got up and walked out to the lounge. She should be happy her son's girlfriend was treating him well. So what if things were still a little awkward between herself and Zoe? They were still getting to know each other. It was bound to take time.

· · ·

ON TUESDAY MORNING, Prudence woke annoyingly early. After an unsuccessful lie-in, she packed her swimming bag, then took Bob for his morning walk. As she was coming back, she met Nathan on the footpath. He reached down and patted Bob on the head.

"Can I borrow the car, Mum?"

"Sorry, I need it today."

"Never mind then. See you later, Mum!"

"Wait! You've got a bit of jam on your cheek!"

He wiped his face and headed off in the direction of the uni.

Prudence went inside and found Zoe in the kitchen, tapping away on her phone while she nursed a cup of tea.

"Morning!" Prudence called out to her. Zoe didn't respond. Perhaps she hadn't heard. "I'm just off to the pool," she called.

She grabbed her swimming bag and headed off to the car, her mind occupied with the details of the coffee morning she was planning. The proceeds were going towards the refurbishment of the children's ward—one of the many things she'd never had time to do while she was working.

The pool was quiet when she arrived. There was only one other person around, a competitive swimmer zooming up and down the fast lane. Prudence preferred a more leisurely pace. She eased in, taking a moment to acclimatise before she began to swim. There was something incredibly relaxing about bobbing up and down in the water. It always made her feel calm.

She swam her customary twenty lengths, then paused at the end to get her breath back.

It was cold when she climbed out and she wished she'd thought to leave her towel by the pool the way she sometimes did. Shaking with cold, she walked through to the changing rooms and opened her locker. She pulled out her bag and looked inside, expecting to find her towel. It wasn't there.

5

PRUDENCE

Prudence was dripping wet with nothing but her clean clothes to dry herself on. She pulled out her cardigan and used it to pat herself down, but the material was useless. Shivering hard, she turned and noticed the hand dryer. She walked over to it and attempted to dry herself with a blast of hot air. It took several more blasts before she was remotely dry, but all the time she couldn't think how she'd been so careless. How had she forgotten to put her towel in the bag? Had she taken it out when she put the shampoo in and somehow left it on her bed? She thought back, but the image wouldn't come. It was ridiculous. She must be getting forgetful in her old age.

Grumpily, she pulled on her clothes. They clung to her damp body and water dripped down her back from her hair. She didn't even have a coat to cover herself with as she walked out of the changing rooms. A woman she knew waved to her as she traipsed through the car park and she forced herself to smile, but she didn't feel remotely cheerful. It was only nine AM, and her day was already ruined.

· · ·

ZOE WAS SITTING in the lounge when she got home. She had her books out on the table and looked like she was studying, but Prudence wondered. It occurred to her that she might be sitting there so that she'd have a good view of her when she walked through the door.

"Nice swim?"

She met Zoe's eyes. She was wearing sparkly purple eyeliner and her eyes seemed to twinkle more than usual. Prudence stopped short.

"Have you seen my towel?"

"Your towel?"

Prudence maintained eye contact but Zoe did not break. She merely clicked her pen and smiled. "I've no idea what you did with your towel, but the kettle's warm if you want some tea. You look kind of cold."

Prudence trudged upstairs and found her missing towel lying on her bedroom floor. She picked it up and stared at it, trying to imagine how it had got there. How could it have just fallen out of the bag like that? She had zipped it up. But the other possibility seemed too crazy. Why would Zoe mess with her like that? Was that her idea of a joke? It seemed pretty childish. And if it was a joke, why hadn't she come clean?

She glanced at the clock. Damn! She was supposed to pick up the tables from the custodian who looked after the town hall. She had to get them this morning because the woman was due to go on holiday. She had planned on doing it on her way back from the pool, but with all the trouble with the towel she had forgotten. With a sigh, she headed back downstairs and out to the car.

The custodian insisted on making Prudence a cup of tea and Prudence accepted, even though she was still cold and grouchy, and she could feel her hair going frizzy. She drank the tea politely and listened as the old woman blabbered on. She kept saying how busy she was and how much she still had to do, and yet every time Prudence made a move to leave, she started talking again.

"I really must be going," Prudence eventually said and stood up with purpose.

"Right, well I suppose I'd better help you with those tables then, although my back's not very good. If you could wait another ten minutes, my son will be here and he could help you."

Prudence gritted her teeth. She was beginning to feel like she was never going to leave.

By the time she got home, she was knackered. She left the tables in the car and opened the front door. Bob shuffled over to her, and she bent down to pet his furry head. She took a step into the lounge and looked around. Something was missing.

"Where's the coffee table?"

She looked at Bob and Bob looked back at her, his large almond eyes wide. Had they been burgled? Her eyes went to the TV, but it was still there, as were her antique elephant figurines. She turned and looked at the mantlepiece. What was her house plant doing up there? She marched into the kitchen and found her cactus had been moved from the windowsill to goodness knows where. What was going on?

She heard a movement upstairs.

"Nathan?" she called. "Zoe?"

Nobody answered, but Prudence wasn't in the mood to be messed about. She stormed up the stairs, with Bob hot on her heels, and rapped on Nathan's door. No answer.

"I'm coming in," she announced and threw the door open. Zoe was sitting at the desk, with her headphones in, but Prudence had a feeling she'd only just sat down. Her suspicions were confirmed by the fact that the laptop screensaver was on.

Zoe swivelled round to face her and dutifully unplugged one ear. "Can I help you?"

"Where's my coffee table?"

Zoe met her eyes. "The edges were sharp."

"Where is it?"

"I gave it to a couple of nice men from the Red Cross. They were doing a collection this morning."

"You gave them my coffee table?"

Zoe pressed her lips together. "The edges were sharp," she said again. "Don't you see? It would be a hazard for the baby."

Prudence looked into her eyes, but she was met with a blank stare.

"It was a normal coffee table. My coffee table. I rather liked it."

Zoe bit her lip "I can call and ask them to bring it back if you want? They'll be out collecting more stuff this morning, but they should be able to ..."

"I'll do it," Prudence growled. "Did you get a phone number?"

"No, sorry. I didn't think you'd want to take back the donation."

Prudence clenched her fists. "In future, kindly ask me before you give away my possessions," she said, and turned on her heel. She stormed out of the room and stood in the hallway, her chest heaving. Her heart was beating a little too fast and she felt pressure in her nose. She kept her fists clenched as she stomped back down the stairs to the lounge. Bob watched her with concerned eyes.

What was Zoe playing at? First the towel, and now her table. Didn't she want to live under her roof? If so, she only had to say so. No one was making her stay. In fact, Prudence was already regretting letting her move in. If it wasn't for the fact that she was carrying her grandchild. *Potential* grandchild ...

Bob gave a little whine and she reached out to pet him. His fur felt a little tangled. Where was the comb? She'd left it on the table. The table that was no longer there.

"It's really spacious, isn't it?" Nathan said, looking around the room. "I never realised how big the lounge was before. It always felt a little ... cluttered."

He was taking Zoe's side. Prudence couldn't believe it. When she told him about the table, she'd expected shock and outrage. She'd have settled for mild annoyance. But he didn't seem the least bit perturbed.

"The plant looks good there too," he said, looking at the mantelpiece. "It makes sense because the baby won't be able to reach up there to pull it down."

"The baby's not even born yet," she reminded him.

"I know, but it doesn't hurt to be prepared."

Prudence drew in a breath and walked quickly from the room. He was siding with Zoe and there was nothing she could do about it. It had taken her all afternoon to track down the table. It had been driven halfway to Derby by the time she got through to the driver and she had to pay to get it returned, and even then they wouldn't be coming back this way until Wednesday.

While Nathan raided the kitchen, Prudence slipped out of the house. Bob lumbered after her as she made for the car. She put him on the backseat and drove round to Heidi's.

"Sorry, I wasn't sure if this was one of your working days." She apologised when Heidi answered the door. Heidi worked from home as a typist, transcribing handwritten papers that looked almost illegible and transforming them into neatly written documents that clients could actually read.

Heidi smiled. "It is, but this is a good excuse for a break."

They drifted into the kitchen and Heidi put out a bowl of water for Bob.

"I've got a bone for him if he's allowed?"

"He'd love that, thanks."

While Bob gnawed on his bone, they carried their mugs of tea into the lounge and sat down. Heidi had given her the same mug as always, the one with the dog on it. Heidi herself always had the cat.

"So, how's it going, having love's young dream move in with you?"

"Infuriating," Prudence admitted, stirring sugar into her tea.

"It'll take a while for you and Zoe to get used to each other," Heidi soothed. "She seems like a good kid."

"Do you think? She barely says a word to me most of the time. And then this morning I think she hid my towel."

Heidi's lips twitched. "Are you sure about that?"

"I'm serious. I think she took it out of my swimming bag. And then she rearranged my furniture and threw out my coffee table."

"That old driftwood thing?"

"I happen to be very fond of that table."

"Didn't you pick it up at a jumble sale?"

"Zoe reckons the edges are sharp."

"She's looking out for the baby."

"Maybe, but she should have asked me first. The worst part is that Nathan took her side."

Heidi smiled. "Well, of course he's going to take her side. She's his girlfriend."

Prudence took a large gulp of her tea. It all sounded so petty when she said the words out loud.

"I'm just not sure about Zoe," she said. "I feel like she's

one person when Nathan's around and another with me. It really does feel like she's deliberately trying to annoy me. I don't know why she would do that, since she's a guest in our house, but I don't know what else to think. She can't put a foot wrong according to Nathan, so the more I criticise her, the more I come off as the bad guy."

"Don't then."

"Don't what?"

"Criticise. Just do your best to get along with her. If there is something up with Zoe, she'll slip up eventually. But I honestly think you're judging her too harshly." She glanced at her watch. "Right, well, I hate to rush you out the door but I've got a Zoom meeting with the boss in ten minutes."

"That's alright, I'll show myself out."

Prudence didn't feel much like returning home. It was nice out, warm with a cool breeze, so she drove to the dog park.

Bob shuffled along beside her as she walked into the park. It was a little more crowded than it had been the last time. She spotted three little poodles in bright pastel colours. She could never understand why people dyed their dogs' fur like that. Their natural colouring was so beautiful.

"Fancy seeing you here again!"

She turned and saw the little dog and his owner. The dog wore a red necktie, and the owner wore a scarf in the same shade.

"Sniffy, isn't it?" she said.

"And your dog's Bob? Sorry, I didn't catch your name ..."

"Prudence."

"Hi, I'm Charlie."

He looked like a Charlie. His ears were on the big side and he had a crooked front tooth, but there was something rather disarming about his smile.

"So how's your week been? I bet it's great being retired.
You get to be your own boss."

"Yeah, it's great!"

"I bet it is! Got big plans for the weekend?"

Prudence bit back a laugh. All she had was a big pile of
laundry. Now that she had all the time in the world, she no
longer felt the motivation to get a load of washing going every
morning. In the space of a few short days, the laundry basket
was overflowing and she bet Zoe and Nathan had even more
in their room. Not that she had to do all their washing. They
were soon to be parents, after all. If they couldn't do it by now,
then it was about time they learnt.

"I'm probably going to do something with my friend
Heidi," she said, not wanting to sound like a total loser. "We
get together most weekends."

He perked up. "No husband then? No partner?"

"Not at the moment, no."

Not in a very long time, if she was honest.

He darted down the hill a little, to check on Sniffy, who
was growling at a much larger dachshund.

"It's okay, he's very tame," the owner of the dachshund
called.

"My Sniffy's a bit of a terror," Charlie apologised, calling
his little dog to heel.

Once the crisis was averted, he turned back to Prudence.
"I feel like I know you from somewhere. Didn't you used to go
to the cricket club?"

"My son did. Nathan. He's eighteen now."

"You don't look old enough to have a son that age."

Prudence blushed. After years of being the oldest parent
at the school gates, that was good to hear. Charlie stuck his
hands in his pockets and traced a circle in the dirt with his
foot.

"You know, there's a new Italian place in town. Two doors

down from the Fox and Hound. Do you like that kind of food? Pasta and pizza and stuff?"

She met his eye. "I like it very much."

"I like trying out new places, but it would be nice to have someone to go with." He looked suddenly shy.

"Is that an invitation?" she asked.

"If you're not too busy?"

She smiled. "That sounds very nice, thank you."

"Let me give you my number. You can text me your address. I'll pick you up Friday at eight."

Perhaps it wasn't the best idea to swap numbers with a total stranger, but she liked Charlie. He was very easy to talk to. She had a feeling they were going to have a fun night. And she couldn't wait to tell Heidi. Her retirement was getting off to a good start after all.

ZOE WAS TALKING on the landline when Prudence got in. Prudence was surprised she knew how to work it. Her generation seemed surgically attached to their mobiles. Perhaps she'd twigged that it was cheaper. She set her bag down in the hall and changed into her slippers.

"I know what I'm doing," she heard Zoe say, as she walked into the lounge. Zoe glanced cat-like at Prudence. She had the phone cradled against her ear. She appeared to be listening intently.

"Of course, you'll be the first to know," she said hurriedly. "Okay, okay. Got to go."

"Everything okay?" Prudence asked as Zoe set down the phone.

Zoe looked flustered. Her forehead furrowed. "Stop fussing over me, will you? I already have a mum. I don't need another one."

Prudence stared at her for a moment, but before she

could think of a suitable response Zoe had retreated up the stairs to Nathan's room.

Prudence stood at the bottom of the stairs, mentally rehearsing things to say. Should she go after Zoe and get her to explain her little outburst? No, she should give her a chance to cool off. The girl clearly had issues.

6

ZOE

From: Zoe Nithercott <Zoe.Nithercott@lbro.ac.uk>
To: Ted Nithercott <Edward.Nithercott@gmail.com>
Subject: Keeping her on her toes

Dad,

I actually quite admire Prudence. I mean, she's living the
dream, isn't she? She's retired early and she doesn't rely on
any man. She's got her own money, and she runs her own life.
What more would any woman want? She needs to watch her
brain doesn't go completely to mush now though. That
happens sometimes, doesn't it? People stop working and they
let themselves go. They end up having a heart attack or a
stroke or something. Well, I won't let that happen to her. I'm
putting her through the wringer. It has to be done.

This morning, I pranked her by taking the towel out of her
swimming bag. She looked like a drowned rat when she came

home from the pool. She asked me about it but I pretended I had no idea what she was talking about, so with any luck she'll think she's going senile. Oh, and I moved all her furniture around. She had this crappy little coffee table that looked like it had been carved out of an old beer barrel. It was really minging and would probably give you a splinter if you touched the side of it, so I gave it away.

Prudence was fuming. You should have seen her face. Then she ratted me out to Nathan, but he agreed with me that the table was a hazard. I'm so proud of him. It proves he really loves me. He has passed the test. Prudence on the other hand does not like being put in her place. She keeps interrupting me whenever I try to study. It's really annoying and I'm sure she only does it to be nosey. She keeps looking at me like she's trying to see inside my brain. Little does she know I've only just begun.

Oh, and Dad! I'm finally showing! I look like a total porker. I was thinking the other day that it would be nice if the baby had your eyes, or your dimple or something. I hope to god it won't take after Jason. That would be just my luck. I'm getting really nervous about the birth now. I can't stop thinking about it. I really hope it all goes to plan.

Right, well got to go now. Lots to do. I need to prepare for every contingency. Hopefully we won't have to resort to the worst scenario, but I can't leave anything to chance.

Love you loads,

Zoe xxx

7

PRUDENCE

Prudence went to the fridge and opened it. She was about to reach for a yoghurt when something cold and metal slid off the top and hit her on the head, then fell to the floor with a clatter. She raised a hand to her forehead. There was no blood but it felt tender. Her gaze dropped to examine the object. Her stainless steel mixing bowls! She normally kept them stacked on top of the fridge, but at the back, out of the way. Not poised so they would fall off and bash her when she opened the fridge door. Was she being totally paranoid, or had Zoe moved them there on purpose?

She set them on the counter and looked at them, as if expecting them to speak. Perhaps Zoe had used them and just been a little thoughtless when she put them back? But Zoe had barely cooked anything since she had moved in, not unless Nathan was involved. She definitely wasn't the domesticated type. It didn't make any sense.

Troubled, she walked back towards the lounge. She could confront Zoe now, but Nathan was upstairs, taking a shower. Perhaps it would be better to wait until he came down. She needed to think about what she was going to say. Because even in her own head, it sounded kind of ridiculous.

When she heard Nathan on the stairs, she rushed to speak to him before Zoe got in first.

"Nathan," she said. "You won't believe what—"

But Nathan wasn't even listening to her. He was looking behind her. "Zoe? What is it?"

"I think the baby just kicked!"

Nathan stepped towards her and pressed his hand to Zoe's stomach. "I felt it!" He looked at Prudence. "You have to feel it too."

Prudence hesitated. "May I?"

Zoe nodded and she pressed her hand to Zoe's stomach. She held her breath and waited and waited but nothing happened. It felt a little awkward standing there with her hand on Zoe's belly. Maybe she should take it away. Maybe Zoe and Nathan had imagined it. It was easy to mistake a bout of ... then she felt it, a strong little kick. She could almost feel the outline of a tiny foot.

"Oh, wow!" She probably should have removed her hand, but then it came again. A real, solid little kick. "I reckon you've got yourself a little footballer there!"

Tears shone in her eyes as she looked at Nathan and Zoe. Their eyes were bright too. Nathan hugged her, and she hugged him back. Zoe, too.

"And again!" Zoe shrieked. They were all grinning, their former animosity forgotten.

"Hey, Mum, what did you do to your head?" Nathan asked. "You've got a big bruise on your forehead."

Prudence looked at Zoe, but the girl gave no indication that she'd had anything to do with it.

"Oh, this?" she said, touching her tender forehead. "I ... knocked it on the cupboard door."

Nathan's grin returned. "Take it easy, Mum, or we're going to have to put you in an old people's home."

PRUDENCE SAT with Heidi in the beer garden at the Fox and Hound. It was a cool evening, but they had Bob warming their feet and a bucket of Prosecco warming their insides.

"Someone moved my mixing bowls," she told Heidi, her voice a little thick. "If it wasn't Zoe, then who the hell did it?"

"Maybe Zoe did move your mixing bowls," Heidi said. "You did say she'd been rearranging the furniture. Sounds like she's nesting."

"Nesting?"

"Yeah, a lot of women do it when they're expecting."

"I never did."

Heidi ran a hand through her hair. "I really think she just wants to feel more at home in your house. I mean, think about it, it's been just you and Nathan for so many years. It must be hard for her to try and slot herself into your family."

"But we don't even know for sure that the baby is Nathan's," Prudence said. "Her own mother told me that Zoe had had a lot of boyfriends before him. What if she got pregnant by one of them and now she's trying to pass it off as his?"

"Why would she do that?"

"Well, I ... we have a nice house. Maybe she wants it."

Heidi burst out laughing. "Honestly, Pru. Do you really think Zoe wants your council house? It's not like she can bump you off and inherit it."

"There's my pension," Prudence said obstinately.

"Can you hear yourself? Zoe seems like a capable young woman and she has her own home to go back to if she needs help raising the baby."

Prudence bit her lip. "I just feel like we're walking into some kind of trap."

Heidi leaned closer. "Do you know what I think?"

"Tell me."

"I think your insecurities about Zoe have something to do with your own situation with Nathan."

"What situation?"

"You know what I mean."

"No, I don't."

Heidi looked at her. "I was there, remember? I know how anxious you were. Your biological clock was ticking and you thought it was never going to happen for you. You were never going to meet Mr Right."

"I didn't need him, as it turned out."

"No, Frank wasn't interested in becoming a father, if I recall. But you knew that when you got pregnant."

Prudence picked up her glass. "I didn't need anything from him. Still don't."

"Except for Nathan. That wasn't quite the accident you made it out to be, was it?"

Prudence paused her glass halfway to her mouth.

"You don't have to lie to me, Prudence. You were desperate for a baby, and then bam, you were pregnant. You'd only been seeing the bloke a couple of months."

"It was an accident. I forgot to take the pill."

"Forgot my arse. But you don't have to explain it to me. It's all worked out for the best, hasn't it?"

Prudence sat back in her chair. That was the trouble with old friends. Sometimes they knew you better than you knew yourself. It wasn't just Heidi she'd lied to. For all these years, she'd believed her own lies. Because it wasn't just that night she'd forgotten her pill. She'd been downright careless. She had tricked Frank into becoming a father, and deep down she had thought that once the baby was born, he would want to be a part of it. She would have given anything to give Nathan a father. Frank had seemed like the ideal candidate. He had been handsome, intelligent and funny. But fatherhood had never been anywhere on his agenda. It was a pity about that, because no other relationship had ever come close to that one. She had sacrificed the only man she'd ever loved in order to become a mother. It had been worth it, though. Nathan was her world.

"It's alright, I'm not judging you." Heidi pulled her into a tight hug, and she exhaled sharply. What if Heidi was right, though? What if she was judging Zoe by her own warped standards?

8

PRUDENCE

Prudence decided to wear her favourite red blouse with black jeans for her dinner date on Friday night. Heidi thought she should wear a dress, but Prudence didn't want to look like she was trying too hard. All the same, she showered, blow-dried her hair and carefully applied make-up before Heidi arrived to inspect the result.

"Stunning," she proclaimed, popping open a bottle of cava. "But your outfit needs something. What about some earrings?"

She delved into Prudence's jewellery box and chose a pair of sparkling faux emeralds that Prudence had last worn a good five or ten years before. Prudence cleaned them before she put them on. Heidi was right – they completed her look nicely. Heidi settled in the armchair next to Prudence's bed and switched on some music. Zoe wandered past at that moment and threw them both a curious look.

"Get in here and tell Prudence how gorgeous she looks!" Heidi called out.

Zoe stopped, startled. She looked at Prudence and a smile

broke like a wave across her face. "You do look pretty," she said.

Heidi patted the bed. "Come on in. Take a seat. We were just about to choose what colour nail varnish Prudence should wear."

Prudence shot her a look. "We were?"

"Of course. You can't go out on a date with plain nails."

She held up the bottle of cava. "Would you like a glass, Zoe?"

"No, I'd better not."

"I've got some non-alcoholic fizz in the fridge. I'll get you a glass while you find a good nail polish for Prudence."

Prudence thought Zoe would make an excuse to leave, but instead she smiled and settled herself on the bed.

"I think this champagne colour would look classy," she told Prudence. "You don't want anything too bright with that top."

Zoe was right. She didn't.

Heidi returned with Zoe's drink and the next thing Prudence knew, Zoe was doing her nails for her. She was good at it, too. On the rare occasions that Prudence did her nails she always went over the lines and needed to dab off a little of the excess, but Zoe's work was perfection.

"My mum trained me when I was little," Zoe said with a smile. "I've saved her thousands on manicurists over the years."

"She must be paying out again now," Prudence said.

Zoe laughed. "I doubt it. She's probably training up one of the neighbours' kids to take over."

Heidi glanced at her watch. "What time did Charlie say he was picking you up?"

"Eight," Prudence said, blowing on her nails. She hoped they'd be ready in time. It would be a bit awkward having tacky nails on her date. What if he wanted to hold her hand?

She felt a little shiver of anticipation at the thought. She wasn't sure how she felt about Charlie yet. He seemed fun. A little bit scruffy, but charming in a laid-back way. She wondered if he'd bothered to put on a nice shirt or if he'd be in the same casual T-shirts he'd worn at the dog park.

"Is there any more of that non-alcoholic wine?" Zoe asked.

"The bottle's in the fridge," Heidi said. "Help yourself."

"Thanks." Zoe hopped off the bed and headed out the door with her empty glass.

Prudence waited a moment, then leaned over to Heidi. "She's not normally like this, you know."

"Like what?"

"Chatty. I barely get a word out of her when Nathan's not around."

"Maybe she's shy."

Prudence thought of the look Zoe had given her the other day. "I don't think that's it."

Zoe returned, her glass now full and Heidi made them both listen to a digitally remastered ABBA song on her phone.

"What did you think?" she asked, once the song ended.

"That he'll be here any minute." Prudence felt a tingle of nerves. She didn't know why she felt this way. This was just a date, with a man she hardly knew. The stakes weren't that high. It wasn't like she was looking for a relationship. She was fine on her own. She was—

"Stop looking at the time," Heidi interrupted. "A watched clock never boils."

"What are you on about?" Zoe asked.

"The younger generation don't even wear watches," Heidi observed. "That's why they're so laid-back about the time."

"Shouldn't he be here by now?" Prudence asked. The feeling was starting to gnaw at her stomach.

"You've got his number, haven't you? Why don't you call him?"

"He'll think I'm impatient!"

"So you should be. He's definitely late."

"Maybe he can't find a parking space."

Heidi changed the music, putting on some other old favourites that Zoe had probably never heard before. To Zoe's credit, she didn't slam the music the way Nathan would have, had he been home. He loved to rib her about her taste. Prudence tried not to look at her watch, but it was impossible not to notice the passing of time, until Heidi said:

"He's twenty minutes late. Don't you think you ought to call him?"

Prudence went downstairs to the kitchen and checked her mobile phone. There were no missed calls. She'd also given him her landline so it wasn't like he couldn't contact her. She went to the window and looked out. The road was quiet, not a soul outside. It dawned on her that he wasn't coming.

"Just call him."

She turned and saw Heidi watching her with a concerned expression.

"Fuck him!" Zoe said. "He's almost half an hour late, Prudence. Don't waste your breath."

Prudence glanced at Heidi, who gave a little shrug. "It's one thing to be late but if he can't be bothered to ring and let you know, then I'm inclined to agree with Zoe. If he's this sloppy on a first date, then he might not be worth your time."

Prudence stared at the phone, willing it to ring, but another minute passed and it didn't. She reached for the phone and held it for a moment. She was half inclined to give him a piece of her mind, but in the end she set it down again. Taking one last glance out the window, she pulled a fresh bottle of wine from the fridge and popped the cork.

"That's the spirit," said Heidi, holding out her glass for a top-up. They sat down at the kitchen table and listened to some more music, while Zoe grabbed a bowl of ice cream and retreated to her room.

A WAFT of toast drifted up to Prudence. She was awake now, but instinct told her to keep her eyes closed. She heard muffled voices followed by the bang of the front door. Even through her closed eyes, the sun was too bright, streaming in the bedroom window. She must have forgotten to close her curtains. The house fell silent. Zoe and Nathan must have gone out. She should make the most of her quiet time. She opened her eyes, and the throbbing sensation grew worse. Ugh, how much had she drunk last night?

Now she was awake, she was filled with a need she couldn't ignore. She threw back her duvet and stumbled towards the bathroom. She sat down heavily on the toilet. The room spun as she emptied her bladder.

The throbbing worsened as she altered her position. She had a memory. *Charlie. Her date.* She finished in the bathroom and walked shakily out into the hallway. There was a bottle of Lucozade and a glass positioned by the bed. Heidi must have left it for her. She opened it and took a long swig, without bothering to pour it into the glass. Then she crawled back into bed and pulled the covers up to her chin. She tried to go back to sleep, but her headache felt worse when she laid down, so she opened her eyes again, only now noticing the packet of aspirin. Heidi thought of everything.

She took two and swallowed them down with a shudder, then reached for the remote. Daytime TV was all she was going to be good for today. She flicked to a *True Crime* marathon and watched as the police hunted down murderer after murderer. For some reason she found that calming.

She was starting to feel a little more human by the time

she'd watched a few episodes, and she was aware of feeling hungry. She stuck an experimental leg out of the bed and then the other. She was a little steadier on her feet now. Steady enough to risk the stairs anyway.

She found Bob asleep in the kitchen. His bowl was empty, so she fed him just in case. She popped some bread in the toaster while Bob hoovered down his meal. She was sure Nathan would have already fed him, but Bob was quite the actor.

She noticed her mobile phone plugged into the wall and reached for it. To her disappointment, there was no word from Charlie. What was going on? Had he completely forgotten? She didn't think it was possible. You didn't ask someone out and then forget. Unless he'd got the day wrong? But he'd have to be pretty scatty if that was the case.

The toast popped and she continued to stare at the phone. What if something had happened to Charlie? What if he was right now lying in a ditch waiting for the emergency services to rescue him? *What if she was the only person who knew he was missing?*

She reached for the phone and brought up his number. She was going to have to call him, if only to put her mind at rest.

"Stop!"

She turned and saw Zoe in the doorway. "I thought you and Nathan were out?"

"Nathan went out. He's covering Bradley's shift at Morrisons. But what are you doing, Prudence? You were going to call him, weren't you?" Zoe's dark eyes were accusing.

Prudence looked at her. "I was, as a matter of fact. Not to give him a second chance. I just want to make sure he's alright."

"He's alright."

"How can you be so certain?"

Zoe lifted her chin. "Because Charlie did actually turn up last night. I'm afraid I had to send him away."

9

PRUDENCE

Something popped in Prudence's head. She thought maybe it was a blood vessel.

"Why? Why would you do that?"

"He arrived while I was in the kitchen," Zoe said. "I saw him swaggering up the path."

"He doesn't swagger."

"Well, he did last night. I could see he was a player. So I went out there and told him you'd changed your mind. I told him you'd had a better offer."

Prudence's stomach lurched. It was all she could do to keep her hands by her sides. She would gladly have strangled Zoe.

"How dare you! It's for me to decide who I go out with. I don't care if you like him or not. My love life is nothing to do with you."

Zoe stared at her for a moment. She seemed surprised by Prudence's reaction. "I was testing him for you to see if he was good enough."

Prudence took a step towards her. "You were meddling,"

she snarled. Then she strode out of the kitchen, not trusting herself to stay a moment longer.

She stomped back up the stairs to her room, her heart pounding. She was so angry she wanted to punch someone, preferably Zoe. She collapsed back on the bed and looked up at the TV. She'd forgotten her toast and now was ravenously hungry. But she couldn't go back down until Zoe had finished in the kitchen. She didn't trust herself not to say something she would regret.

She reached for the phone by her bed. She had to call Charlie and apologise for Zoe's behaviour.

The phone rang for a couple of minutes but she held firm. If she was him, she wouldn't want to pick up either. It went through to his answerphone:

"Hi, this is Charlie. If you want you can leave me a message, but I don't really listen to them anyway—"

"Charlie? This is Prudence. I ... I just wanted to explain—"

"Prudence?" Suddenly Charlie himself was on the line. *Oh god, what should she say?*

"Charlie, I'm so sorry about yesterday. I didn't know my son's girlfriend had sent you away. She had no right to do that—"

"I was surprised, to say the least," he said. "I thought I'd been dumped in just about every way possible but that was a new one on me. I didn't even get my foot in the door."

"I know and I'm sorry."

"Not half as sorry as I am. I'd even ironed my best Hawaiian shirt for the occasion."

She smiled. "I wish I'd seen that."

"So you honestly didn't send her out to warn me off?"

"Why would I do that?"

"I don't know. I thought perhaps you'd changed your mind."

"Well, I hadn't. I was looking forward to it."

"Me too. So, do you want to try again?" she asked hopefully.

There was a pause.

"You know what, Prudence? I like you. You're a woman after my own heart, but I have to be honest here. I was just looking for a little fun and now, knowing more about your family situation, I'm not sure I knew what I was letting myself in for. I think, if it's okay with you, I'd prefer to just stay friends. I don't do complicated, and your life right now seems about as complicated as it gets."

Prudence let all the air out of her lungs with a huge whoosh. She'd really thought they could get past this, but he'd clearly made up his mind and there was no point trying to persuade him otherwise. She'd had one chance and she'd blown it. Or rather Zoe had.

"That's fair enough," she heard herself say lightly. She'd rather die than let him know how much it hurt. She barely knew the man. Like he'd said, it had just been a little fun.

After she hung up she sat in silence. Her head throbbed. Her stomach rumbled and she felt horribly deflated.

By the time Nathan came home, Prudence was engrossed in some old episodes of *Strictly Come Dancing*. She had just eaten three rounds of toast with Marmite. She hadn't even enjoyed the third piece. The Marmite stuck to her teeth.

"Hi, Mum, how was your big night?"

Prudence looked at Zoe. "She sent him away."

"Why?"

Zoe took a step towards Nathan. "You should have seen him, Nathy. He was such a creep. So many red flags."

"Don't you think that was my choice?"

"He made me want to puke, the way he was eyeing me up. He was a total player."

Prudence didn't believe for a moment that Charlie was 'acting like a creep'. It was true, Zoe was young and attractive, but she couldn't see Charlie lusting after her, especially now she was so obviously pregnant. She recalled what Alana had said about Zoe going out with a lot of different boys. She'd obviously been a popular girl, growing up. Perhaps all the attention had swelled her head and she now thought all men fancied her.

"She was just looking out for you, Mum," Nathan said.

"She was playing games," Prudence told him. She got up and went to the fridge. She was sick of him backing Zoe. It seemed she could do no wrong.

"Do you want any help with lunch?" Zoe asked, trailing after her.

"No, thank you," Prudence said stiffly. "I can manage."

LATER, Heidi rang. Prudence took the call in her bedroom. She kept her voice low, not wanting Zoe to listen in. It was ridiculous, having to sneak around like this in her own home.

"Can you believe it? Zoe sent him away. Who does she think she is?"

"It sounds like she was trying to protect you," Heidi said, uncertainly.

"Oh, get a grip!" Prudence snorted. "She's playing games with me, like when she hid my towel that time. Like when she moved the mixing bowls and positioned them so they'd fall on me when I opened the fridge."

Heidi burst out laughing. "Do you know what you sound like? I'm sure Zoe didn't do any of those things. I mean, yes, she should have let you make your own mind up about Charlie, but I'm sure she meant well."

Prudence resisted the urge to hang up on her oldest friend. "We'll have to agree to disagree," she said unhappily.

"Oh, don't be like that. Why don't we go and have a drink at the pub? That'll cheer you up."

Prudence sniffed. "I had more than enough to drink last night, thanks. I think I'll have an early night."

She hung up and immediately felt bad for laying into Heidi. It wasn't her fault Zoe was messing with her. She just wished Heidi would see it from her point of view. Everyone was always so quick to defend Zoe. It was because she was pregnant. No one wanted to upset her. Well, it was driving Prudence bonkers. Zoe was trying to control her life and she wasn't having it.

Bob strained against his lead on Monday morning. He didn't want to walk this way, past the shops. He wanted to run wild in the dog park, but Prudence couldn't face bumping into Charlie. Her cheeks burned as she thought of him. How embarrassing. What must he think of her?

After a boring walk around the neighbourhood, she marched home with purpose. She was soon busy, printing labels and making calls. Forget Charlie. She was determined to make a big success of her coffee morning. She was in the middle of printing off the jam labels when a nasty smell filled the room.

"Oh god, Bob, was that you?"

Bob looked at her with a mischievous grin.

"Did you do that on purpose?"

She turned back to her printing, but the smell was too much to bear.

"Come on," she told him, leading him out to the garden. "You can play out here for a bit."

She worked hard for the next couple of hours, checking off item after item on her list.

"Looks like you're all ready," Nathan said as she piled the last of the jars of jam into her car.

"I think so," she said with a smile.

"Sorry I can't be there. I've got a really important thermo-dynamics tutorial," he said. "But perhaps Zoe could help out if you need an extra pair of hands?"

Prudence was about to refuse but then she bit back her words. Heidi thought the sun shined out of Zoe's arse. Perhaps if she spent a whole afternoon with her, she'd see that she wasn't the sweet young woman she pretended to be. If Zoe was even willing to help out, which was a big if.

"Alright, ask her," she said.

"Really?" Even Nathan looked surprised.

"Really," Prudence said. "I could use the help."

NATHAN WENT INTO THE LOUNGE, where Zoe had sprawled out with her books. Prudence expected Zoe to excuse herself from the coffee morning but instead she seemed pleased to be asked.

"I'd love to help. I've never been to a coffee morning!" she said, which struck Prudence as rather odd. Didn't they have coffee mornings up in Cheshire? More likely they just weren't Alana's cup of tea. She couldn't really picture Zoe's elegant mother sifting through a pile of second-hand jumpers.

THE SKY LOOKED overcast by the time Prudence and Zoe pulled up outside the hall.

"I hope the weather doesn't put people off coming," she commented, as she parked the car.

"Oh, I'm sure it won't," Zoe said doubtfully.

They began unloading, Prudence carrying the tables inside whilst Zoe helped with the jam jars.

There were already a good number of volunteers inside, which was a good sign. The volunteers could buy the jam, even if they didn't get many customers! Most of the volunteers were around Prudence's age, or older. She spotted Heidi standing on a table, putting up the decorations. Good old Heidi, she didn't need anyone to tell her what to do. She just got on and did it. Her old work friends, Jackie and Caroline, zeroed in on Zoe, practically fighting over whose stall she should help out on. Zoe said something and Caroline burst out laughing. Prudence glanced round but Caroline was tight-lipped, like a naughty schoolgirl in assembly.

"Damn, I forgot to buy the squash," Jackie said as she set up the tea point.

Zoe stepped forward. "Would you like me to go and get some from the shop?"

"I'll go with her," Caroline said. "Zoe shouldn't carry anything heavy."

Zoe smiled sweetly and they walked off together.

"What a nice girl," she heard Jackie say.

When Caroline and Zoe returned, they were talking and laughing like old friends. They gave the bottles of squash to Jackie, then finished setting up Caroline's stall, which was selling knitwear and jam.

Once the coffee morning got underway, Prudence was kept busy selling raffle tickets.

She glanced over at the knitwear stall, where Zoe was doing a roaring trade. She'd even managed to flog a set of knitted ties to one old man. No way he was ever going to wear them.

· · ·

"She's a marvel, your Zoe," Jackie said, once the queue died down. "She's really got a way with words, hasn't she?"

Prudence looked towards the door. "Oh, look, Ethel's here!"

Ethel was a local legend. Some people said she was eighty-six. Others put her at over a hundred. All they knew for sure was that she was on her third husband, a sprightly young eighty-year-old with a full head of hair, albeit a bit thinning on the top. Zoe smiled at him, and he floated over to her as if in a dream.

"What you got there, my lovely?"

"Homemade strawberry jam," Zoe said, fluttering her lashes. Was she flirting with the old man?

Prudence watched as Zoe bagged up his purchases. The old man chuckled as he walked away.

A moment later, Zoe rose from her chair. "Exciting announcement, everyone." She paused for effect. "We've officially sold out of jam!"

People clapped and cheered and Zoe danced about in delight.

"Her enthusiasm is just infectious," Jackie commented. "She'd make a great saleswoman, your daughter-in-law."

"She's not my daughter-in-law," Prudence said. "She's just some girl my son got pregnant."

"Prudence!" They all looked shocked.

Prudence stuck out her lower lip like a petulant child.

The crowd dwindled until there were just a handful of people milling around.

"I think we'd better pack up," Prudence said.

Heidi rose from her seat. "I'll lend a hand with the washing-up."

Zoe appeared at her shoulder. "Do you want me to count up all the money? I'm good at maths."

Prudence eyed her warily. "That's okay, I can manage. Why don't you go and help Heidi with the washing-up?"

Zoe looked as if she was going to object, but then she forced her mouth into a saintly smile and did as she was told. Prudence settled at her table and began the laborious job of counting. Actually, she could have done with a second pair of eyes because it was so easy to lose track, but there was no way she was going to trust Zoe with the cash. The girl was a little too interested in money for her liking.

Sensing her mood, her friends backed off while she counted out the takings. They'd raised almost £800. She'd kick in a few quid to make it even. A very good total indeed. She ought to be feeling really pleased, but instead all she could focus on was the laughter coming from the kitchen, where Zoe was holding court with Heidi and Caroline. Her son's girlfriend had them both wrapped around her little finger, and it was driving Prudence insane.

Once they had packed everything away, Prudence and Zoe went out to the car.

"I'll have to stop at the bank on the way home," Prudence told her. She didn't like the thought of having all that money lying about the house.

"Okay," Zoe said, looking out the window. She was still quite cheerful, Prudence thought. Had she actually enjoyed helping out?

Prudence found a parking space in Granby Street.

"I'll walk into the bank with you," Zoe offered.

"No, I'll be fine. You can wait here."

"Oh no, I'd never forgive myself if you got mugged or something. Let me walk with you, Prudence. I'd really feel much better about it."

Prudence forced a laugh. "What would you do against a

robber? You're pregnant and I'm old. If someone threatened us, we'd stand no chance."

Zoe smiled slyly. "I don't know about that, Prudence. I'd put up a pretty good fight. I don't mess around where money's involved."

No, thought Prudence. *I bet you don't.*

Zoe led the way, down a narrow alley and past a nightclub where teenagers had congregated. They wore ripped jeans and spikey neck collars. They were talking and laughing loudly. One of them stared at her as she walked past and she felt her cheeks grow hot.

She was used to young people. She'd dealt with plenty of them working at the hospital. There was nothing to be afraid of, and yet she was very aware of the wads of cash in her handbag, aware also that Zoe had moved in closer.

One of the teenagers yelled something. An empty can clattered to the ground in front of her. Loud, raucous laughter broke out and then another missile came their way. She quickened her step, but Zoe was falling behind. She turned and saw that Zoe had picked up the can and was now stomping towards the group.

"Zoe!" she called, but there was no stopping her. Prudence heard her own breathing, fast and uneven. Zoe lobbed the can back at the group. There was a moment of stunned silence.

Shit.

She picked up her pace, walking as fast as she could. She just hoped Zoe would follow. She could hear them behind her as her foot connected with the stone steps that led up to the bank. She grabbed Zoe's hand and pulled her inside.

There was no queue. Prudence walked up and handed over the money and waited patiently while the teller counted it all out and confirmed the amount.

"Anything else I can do for you today?" she asked when she had finished.

"Er, no. That's it thanks."

Prudence looked nervously at Zoe, who still seemed unconcerned. They walked towards the door and peered out.

"They've gone," Zoe said.

"But have they?" Prudence asked. For all she knew, they could be lying in wait for them round the corner, or down the alley.

"We'll go the long way round," Prudence decided. "We can pop into the deli and pick up some food for dinner. I doubt I'll want to cook anyway."

"OK," Zoe agreed.

Prudence let Zoe choose what they were having for dinner. For someone who was obsessed with money, she had expensive tastes, choosing lamb tagine with avocado and pea risotto. Prudence added a bottle of wine to her basket. After all, she had earned it.

"Oh, they're back!" Zoe exclaimed, as they were about to turn into the car park.

Prudence froze. The teenagers were walking their way. She picked up her pace. She could hear them talking loudly behind her. Then all went quiet.

"They went into Burger King," Zoe said.

"Thank god for that."

THEY DROVE HOME IN SILENCE. Prudence was out of small talk and it seemed Zoe was, too. She put the food and wine in the fridge, then went out to the garden to check on the dog.

"Bob?" she called. "Bob?"

She peered into his kennel, but it was empty. She looked all around. It was a large garden, but not large enough to conceal a dog Bob's size.

"Where the hell is he?"

"Bob!" Prudence shouted, but the dog didn't come. She dashed towards the gate, the tiredness in her bones all but forgotten. The gate was closed, but it was off the latch.

"Bob!"

10

ZOE

From: Zoe Nithercott <Zoe.Nithercott@lbro.ac.uk>
To: Ted Nithercott <Edward.Nithercott@gmail.com>
Subject: Here's the latest...

Dad,

The old prune didn't close her gate properly and now she's blaming me because her dog got out. It just goes to show you how little she trusts me. Anyway, I'm not sorry the dog is gone. All that dog hair made me sneeze like crazy. Besides, we both know no good can come from owning a pet. Mum had a rabbit once and then Grandad took him out to the shed and slaughtered him for Christmas dinner. Meat is food. End of. Keeping animals as pets is cruel.

I feel bad for Nathan though. He really loved that dog. More than I ever realised. This morning when I came out of the shower I found him crying in our room. He's had the dog a long time so I suppose he was really attached. It's the not knowing that he finds hardest to bear. Bob is out there somewhere; we just don't know where. I comforted him as best I could but

I hope he gets over it soon. The baby will be here before we know it. Isn't that all that matters? I still don't really know what I'm doing. It all keeps going round and round in my head and the baby's getting bigger and bigger. A part of me can't wait to meet him. The other part is terrified.

Zoe xxx

11

PRUDENCE

They walked around the neighbourhood for hours. Nathan came home and joined in the search, replacing Zoe, who was tired.

"Maybe he'll find his way home," Zoe said brightly.

"Maybe," Nathan agreed.

"Like hell he will," Prudence muttered.

Nathan turned on her. "Mum?"

Prudence bit her lip. This wasn't the time. "I'm going to check the woods again," she told him. "You go the other way. I'll meet you back at the house."

She walked on, calling and whistling. They ran into a couple of the neighbours, who went out looking with their own dogs, but Bob was nowhere to be seen and Prudence was growing increasingly frantic.

It was late by the time they returned home. Heidi had gone out in her car, driving around the town, but there was no sign of him.

"No news is good news," one of the neighbours said.

Prudence held her tongue. The ache in her stomach was unbearable. It felt physical, that pain. A hard knot had formed in her belly. She'd had Bob for thirteen years. He was almost as dear to her as her own son. The thought of any harm coming to him sent splinters through her heart.

Nathan had started a fire in the hearth when she got in and was poking it with a stick. Zoe sat beside him, quiet and thoughtful, occasionally reaching over to rub his arm. Prudence's cheeks flared with anger. That girl had brought nothing but trouble. They'd been fine before she came along and now her life was full of nasty little surprises, and this one was the worst of all.

"I don't understand how he got out," Nathan said.

"Oh, I think I have a pretty good idea," Prudence said. "You never liked him much, did you, Zoe?"

"I—"

Nathan turned on her. "I know you're upset but don't take it out on Zoe."

"How else would he have got out? The gate was locked. I would never leave it open. And if he'd got out accidentally, the gate would still be open, wouldn't it? But it was closed."

"Maybe the wind shut it?" he suggested.

"And maybe a magical fairy came along. This is bullshit, Nathan. Your girlfriend never liked Bob and now she's got rid of him."

She suddenly realised that Zoe was no longer next to them. She had edged her way to the door and stood there, wide eyed as if she expected them to start throwing things.

Nathan glanced at her and his features softened.

"Mum, enough of this. Zoe didn't do it. I know she didn't. Here, you sit and enjoy the fire. We're going up to bed. We'll get up an hour early in the morning and go out looking for him. With any luck he's just got trapped in someone's outhouse. You know what a silly mutt he can be."

He touched her shoulder gently, and she let him go. He was a good boy, Nathan, but he was no match for Zoe.

· · ·

PRUDENCE SLEPT with Bob's teddy bear close to her heart. It was old and chewed to bits, but Bob had loved that thing and now she did too. There had been no news overnight. She couldn't understand it. A dog Bob's size didn't wander about unnoticed. Especially an Old English Sheepdog. They were a rare breed. People had always commented on Bob, wherever she went. Telling her how gorgeous he was. If no one had seen him, then the most likely explanation was that he had been stolen. She really hoped not. She couldn't bear it.

The morning search was unsuccessful. She called until she was hoarse but there was no reply. Disheartened, she returned to the house. Heidi was waiting for her in the kitchen.

"No luck?"

Prudence shook her head.

"I can't believe it," Heidi said. "Poor old Bob."

"Do you see now what I've been telling you? It has to be Zoe's doing."

Heidi looked at her with troubled eyes. "But why, Prudence? Why would Zoe want to do such a thing? I really think you've got this wrong. You're upset and looking for someone to blame."

"Mum ..."

Nathan filled the doorway. She could never get used to the way he towered over her. He had once been so tiny. When he was first born, she'd held him in the crook of her arm. And now he was a real person with thoughts and feelings, often completely contrary to her own.

"You need to lay off Zoe. She's really upset. In fact, I think you owe her an apology."

Prudence's jaw dropped. "You want me to apologise to Zoe?"

"Yes! She can't even walk into the room without you staring at her, shooting accusing looks her way. It's not fair, Mum. She hasn't done anything."

"How do you know?"

He fixed her with his eyes. "I just know."

ZOE REMAINED UPSTAIRS ALL MORNING, but when she finally came down Prudence noticed the dark shadows under her eyes. She clearly hadn't slept well. Prudence felt a little uneasy. What if she had been too quick to blame Zoe? The girl looked utterly miserable, which she should be if she had let Bob out, but what if she hadn't? Prudence wavered. She hated the idea that she had turned into some kind of dragon mother-in-law, the kind that other women moaned about.

Sod it. She would be the bigger person here.

"Look, Zoe, I'm sorry I was a bit hard on you about the gate. I was just upset. Bob is a very special dog. I realise now that you wouldn't have let him out on purpose, so if you did it accidentally, then I understand."

"I didn't do it."

Prudence bit her lip. She wasn't sure what to think anymore but she couldn't stand to upset Nathan, so for his sake she would make an effort to get along with Zoe.

A knock came at the door. It was Caroline. Her face looked puffy, her nose was red and her eyes shone with tears.

"I think we've found him," she said. "Or rather Sooty found him. On the corner of Belton Road, down by the canal."

Prudence rose to her feet. "Take me to him."

"Are you sure? It's ... not a pretty sight. There's nothing that can be done for him, I'm afraid. He must have been hit pretty badly but there's no sign of the driver."

"I need to see him."

"I'm coming too," Nathan said.

Prudence nodded, grateful for her son's support.

Nathan turned and looked at Zoe. "You wait here. This isn't something you'd want to see."

They walked in silence. After a few minutes, Prudence heard footsteps behind them. Instinctively she turned. It was Zoe. Of course, it was. She couldn't leave them alone for a minute, not even now.

"I wanted to be with you," Zoe said, sounding out of breath.

Prudence shook with fury. Hadn't she already done enough? She stomped on in silence. She couldn't think about Zoe now. She had to get to Bob. Caroline pointed out the spot where she'd found him, then she stepped back, as if she couldn't bear to look.

Bob lay motionless by the side of the road. Prudence quickened her step.

"Bob? Bob, I'm here, boy. You're going to be just fine."

He let out the smallest of moans and she drew him to her. He knew she was there; at least, she hoped he did. She breathed in his soft, doggy fur. His eyes were open but unseeing, and he smelled wrong. The life was seeping out of his battered body.

"Oh god, Bob!"

She held him and wept, her tears mingling with the dirt on his fur. Then Nathan was on the ground too, the two of them hugging him, hugging each other.

Zoe stood apart from them. Even in the depths of her grief, Prudence felt her gaze, interested and alert. She turned slowly and looked at her. Zoe's mouth hung open, as though she was surprised to witness their pain.

"It must have been a hit and run," Nathan commented. "Did you see the skid marks in the road?"

Prudence nodded. "Some arsehole hit him and didn't even stop."

How long had he lain there, injured and bleeding? Thinking they were never going to come.

Prudence couldn't take it anymore. She swept him up in her arms and carried him as gently as she could home.

By the time they reached the house, Bob had stopped moving altogether. Prudence listened carefully, but she couldn't find a pulse.

"He's not in pain anymore," she told Nathan.

Nathan buried his head in Zoe's shoulder and the pair of them wept together. Why was Zoe crying? She hadn't even liked Bob. The dog's eyes were closed now, his body still. She covered him with a blanket and traced a hand through his woolly fur. Then she stepped outside into the garden to cry.

NATHAN DUG a hole down near the apple tree. There was a bit of land there she'd let go wild. It was supposed to attract bees, but it was currently a feral wasteland ruled by nettles. Within a couple of hours he had cleared it and created a resting place for Bob. Prudence went to the garden centre and bought a dog statue that she'd noticed before. It looked somewhat like Bob and she'd always liked it but hadn't allowed herself the extravagance. Now it seemed fitting. They would look at that statue and always think of Bob.

They buried him and stood in silence for a moment. Nathan linked hands with Prudence on one side and Zoe on the other. He spoke beautifully, telling the story of the day Bob had bounded into their lives. Hard to believe it now but he'd been the runt of the litter. The dog no one else had wanted.

Prudence dabbed her eyes. "What fools they all were. He was the best dog I ever had."

She heard a strangled sound and flicked her eyes to see Zoe sobbing into Nathan's shoulder. Was she for real, or was she putting it on? Prudence couldn't tell. When she came up for air, her eyes looked red, but that might have been because she'd been rubbing them so much. Nathan seemed to buy it, though. He and Zoe headed back into the house and up to their room, leaving Prudence feeling broken and empty.

"Have any witnesses come forward?" Heidi asked later.

"No. I even posted on the community board. No one saw anything. Or if they did, they're not saying. I just don't understand it. How could they leave him on the side of the road like that?"

"They probably didn't want to pay the vet bills," Heidi guessed.

"We might have been able to save him if we'd got to him quicker."

It didn't bear thinking about.

"How's Nathan taking it?"

"He's upset, of course, and Zoe's been crying buckets. I'm not sure why. She doesn't even like dogs."

"It's probably the pregnancy hormones," Heidi said.

"Hmm ..."

Prudence didn't buy it. Zoe was feeling guilty for killing her dog.

"Come on, it's not like she knocked him down herself," Heidi reasoned. "She doesn't even drive, so at the most she might have left the gate open. If she did, I bet she feels really bad about it. No wonder she hasn't said anything."

Prudence wanted to scream. "Why are you always standing up for her?"

"I'm not. I'm just trying to be the voice of reason. Whatever your feelings about Zoe, you need to get along with her. She's having your grandchild."

"I'm not even sure about that," Prudence grumbled.

"What do you mean?"

"How do I even know the baby is his?" she said. "For all I know, she was pregnant when she met him. What if she got knocked up by some boy who wasn't father material? Or what if she doesn't even know who the father is? She didn't even know how far along she was until she had the dating scan."

"That happens to lots of women," Heidi argued. "I really think you ought to give Zoe the benefit of the doubt."

"But that's just it, I can't. I really need to know if that's Nathan's baby she's carrying, because if it isn't, she can fuck right off home to her mum."

"So what are you going to do?"

"I'm going to send off for a paternity test. If it's Nathan's, then I'll just have to learn to live with Zoe. But if it isn't, she's out on her ear as soon as the baby is born."

12

ZOE

From: Zoe Nithercott <Zoe.Nithercott@lbro.ac.uk>
To: Ted Nithercott <Edward.Nithercott@gmail.com>
Subject: Tomorrow

Dad,

I know what death smells like now. Nathan's dog got run over
and it was just horrible. Seriously, it was the most messed up
thing I've ever seen in my life. It wasn't my fault, I mean I
suppose I might have left the gate open a teeny bit, but I
didn't think the dog would wander that far. I never thought
that would happen. I just have a habit of fucking things up.
It's not my fault.

I can't say anything to the old prune because she's just
looking for an excuse to chuck me out. And I can't tell Nathan
because he'll hate me. There's nothing I can do about it now.

What's done is done, but I promise I'll do better, Dad. I won't let you down again.

Despite all the drama, I'm feeling less tired now, although I'm starting to resemble a hippo. My clothes don't fit anymore so I'm living in my joggers and borrowing tops from Nathan's wardrobe. His shirts are so much comfier than mine. I don't want to buy too many maternity clothes because it's more important to save. I have almost 3k now but it's no way near enough.

I've been trying really hard not to think too much about the future. It's painful, you know? Everything hinges on tomorrow—all my happiness and my entire future. The baby's future too. I'm so scared but I'm ready. Once I have that scan result, I'll know what I have to do.

Zoe xxx

13

PRUDENCE

"Will you get another dog?" Zoe asked, as she slipped on her shoes.

Prudence swallowed the lump in her throat. "No, I don't think so. Not yet."

She needed time to mourn Bob, and besides, they had a baby coming. It wasn't the time.

Nathan nodded. "It's weird not having him around. I keep expecting him to come bounding up the garden and then I remember and it's just ..."

Prudence stepped towards her son and gave him a tight squeeze. "I know."

Nathan tolerated the hug briefly then went back to packing his bag for uni, cramming in packets of crisps, apples and two ham sandwiches.

"Do you really need all that?" Prudence asked. "I mean, you've got the appointment at three."

"I know."

"Do you want me to come with you?" She tried not to sound too hopeful.

"No, that's okay."

"Alright, then. Are you going to find out what the baby's sex is?"

"No."

"Yes," Zoe said at the exact same time.

Nathan looked confused. "I thought you didn't want to know?"

"Yeah, I know, but I talked to Mum and she's dying to know."

Prudence narrowed her eyes. "Well, what do you want?"

"I think she's right. Then we'll know whether to buy boy clothes or girl clothes."

"If that's what you want," Nathan said.

Zoe nodded. "It is."

"Well, good luck, the pair of you," Prudence said. "I just want to hear the baby's healthy. That's all that really matters."

She watched as they drove off, unable to settle the flutter in her tummy. Despite all her animosity for Zoe, she really felt for her now. She knew what it was like to walk into that room, holding tight to all your hopes and dreams.

She couldn't bear it. She whirled around and grabbed the lead from its hook before she realised what she was doing. No Bob to walk. She knew on some level that she didn't need a dog in order to go for a walk, but walks had been Bob's thing and it wouldn't be the same without him.

She would distract herself by cleaning the house. She'd been incredibly lax since she'd retired and it was starting to show. She scrubbed the bathroom until she could see herself in the taps, then she ran the hoover round all the downstairs rooms, dusting and straightening everything as she went.

Right in the middle of her cleaning frenzy, the phone rang. She dived for it, wiping her dusty hands on her trousers.

"Hello?"

"Oh, hi. This is Alana. Are they back yet?"

"Not yet. I think they'll be about an hour."

"Okay." Alana sounded disappointed.

"I'm sure it will all be fine," Prudence reassured her. "But I'll make sure Zoe gives you a ring as soon as they get in."

"Thank you," Alana said. "I'm sure you're just as excited as me."

"I am." She hesitated. Should she ask her about Zoe's other boyfriends? She tried to find the words, but it felt rude, given the circumstances. And how could Alana even know for sure? The only way she could really know was to wait for the baby to be born.

She said goodbye to Alana and lugged the hoover up the stairs. She stopped in front of Nathan's room. Her son was a grown man now. Should she really be cleaning for him? Maybe not, but she hadn't been in there for weeks and she wanted to see what kind of a state it was in. She pushed open the door and looked inside.

She'd have thought Zoe would have made some kind of impression on the room. At the very least, she'd expected to see perfume bottles and hand lotions and items of underwear or little trinkets lying around, but aside from the suitcase peeking out from under the bed, there was no sign of her son's girlfriend at all. She ventured further in and pulled open one of the drawers. Here were a few of Zoe's textbooks; she could tell by the titles. Heavy tomes on subjects like banking and finance and economics. She heard the front door bang, and she shut the drawer quickly.

She rushed downstairs and took in Nathan's happy face.

"The baby's doing well, Mum. Do you want to see the scan picture?"

"Of course I do." She glanced at Zoe, who still looked a little tense. Perhaps the good news hadn't sunk in yet. She remembered how nervous she'd been when she'd had her scans with Nathan.

Prudence took the picture and looked at it. "Try to relax, Zoe. It all looks good."

She smiled at Zoe, but Zoe didn't smile back, so she tried again. "Were they able to tell you the sex?"

"It's a girl. Mum will be pleased."

"Oh, yes, your mum rang while you were out. I said you'd give her a ring as soon as you got back."

Zoe took out her mobile phone and dialled. "It's a girl, Mum!"

Even Prudence could hear Alana's cry of delight.

"I think she's happy," Nathan said.

Prudence looked at Zoe. "Do tell your mum that they get it wrong sometimes," she cautioned. "I've known a couple of people who thought they were having a girl and it turned out to be a boy!"

Zoe stared at her for a moment, then relayed this to her mum. Once she had finished the call, she and Nathan retreated upstairs to their room. Prudence heard them talking in low voices. Were they arguing again? She couldn't be sure.

They looked very serious when they came back downstairs. They headed for the kitchen, and she heard the opening and closing of the fridge as they made themselves a snack. She didn't mean to be nosey, but she couldn't help but listen in.

"If you think that will work ..." she heard Zoe say.

Nathan murmured something and then Zoe said: "Final resort."

What were they talking about? It all seemed very serious. Unable to hold back any longer, she walked into the kitchen. Nathan was spreading butter on some crackers, while Zoe leaned against the sink. She was so pale, Prudence was concerned.

"Why don't you have a rest?" she suggested gently. "I'll

sort dinner out tonight. I've got a cottage pie in the freezer. We can have that."

Zoe nodded absently and headed up the stairs.

Prudence watched her son as he added a large chunk of cheese to his snack. He looked rather solemn, she thought. Of course, fatherhood was a serious proposition, but oh, so exciting. A little girl. A granddaughter. It was hard not to picture her, with little round cheeks and twinkling eyes.

If the baby was really Nathan's. She kept coming back to that. It was maddening. But there was no real way to know until the baby was born.

"Have you thought of any names?" she asked.

Nathan didn't answer. He put a piece of cheese in his mouth and chewed on it, deep in thought.

"Something wrong?"

He looked up, startled. "What? I'm fine, Mum. All good."

"Are you sure?" she probed. "You're still happy with Zoe?"

"Of course I am. Zoe and the baby are the best things that have ever happened to me."

"Because if you have any doubts, I bought a paternity test. You can take it once the baby is born, just to make sure it's yours and not one of those other boys."

"What other boys?" Nathan snarled. "Look, Mum, I know it's my baby. We don't need any paternity test, so back off, okay?"

ZOE SAT at the kitchen table, studying. She seemed to be going into uni less and less, preferring to work online. Prudence could understand it. In the last few weeks, she had really popped, and Prudence guessed she was more comfortable at home, not to mention the fact that she needed the toilet every five minutes.

While Zoe studied, Prudence went outside to inspect the

garden. She hadn't been out there much since they'd lost Bob.
She still thought of it as his territory. She went down to his
memorial and gazed into the eyes of his statue.

"I miss you, Bob," she said, stroking the stone dog's nose.

As she walked back up the garden, she noticed that the
grass was looking overgrown so she went to the shed and
pulled out the mower. Mowing the lawn was usually Nathan's
job but he'd been working so hard lately, what with his uni
work and his job. She, on the other hand, had nothing but
time.

The mower was a bit heavier than she'd remembered, but
she managed to extract it from the shed. She plugged it in,
but as she reached for the handle, a massive jolt of electricity
shot through her arm. She tried to release her grip, but she
couldn't let go. She held on for what felt like an eternity as
electricity surged through her body.

14

She must have screamed because the back door burst open and Zoe came running out.

"Prudence! Oh my god!"

Zoe ran to the mains and turned it off.

Prudence blinked and dropped to the ground. She still couldn't move her arm – it was like it didn't belong to her. Zoe loomed over her.

"What happened?" She looked deeply concerned, but Prudence shifted away from her. "You're hurt, aren't you? Come on, I'm taking you to A&E."

Zoe disappeared out the gate. Prudence didn't have the strength to stand. She was shaking from head to toe. She heard voices and for a moment she thought it was Nathan, home unexpectedly from uni. But no, it was her quiet neighbour, Jon. The man had lived next door to her for the past sixteen years and she'd never got more than one or two words out of him.

"Jon's kindly offered to drive us to the hospital," Zoe said, sounding a little out of breath.

Prudence felt her cheeks go red. "No, really, that isn't necessary."

Jon looked at her with hawkish, serious eyes. "Sounds like you've had a nasty shock," he said. "I'd really feel better if you'd get yourself checked out."

She started to protest, but then she realised that he was right. She had had a nasty shock and she still couldn't feel her arm. She let Jon help her up and followed him out to his battered red Renault. She climbed in beside him and Zoe got in the back.

"You don't need to come," she told Zoe. "Why don't you go back to your books?"

"I want to make sure you're okay," Zoe said. "What if something happens to you while you're waiting?"

Prudence nodded weakly.

The short drive to the hospital was made in silence. Jon did not switch on the radio, nor did he feel the need to fill the gap with meaningless small talk. Under ordinary circumstances, Prudence would have asked him more about himself and tried to get to know him, but her whole foundation had been shaken and she found his silence oddly comforting.

All the same, she was very aware of Zoe, sitting behind her, breathing down her back. She glanced in the mirror and saw that Zoe was tapping away on her mobile, a frown etched into her face. Zoe threw a glance her way and Prudence concentrated her gaze on the road.

"How's the arm?" Jon said, as they neared the hospital.

"Getting better," Prudence lied. It wasn't. She had to keep checking to make sure it was still there.

Jon dropped them off outside the hospital and Zoe insisted on taking Prudence's good arm to help her up the steps. Prudence was still a little shaky, so she accepted her help without a word.

"You must know everyone," Zoe said, as they stepped

inside. Prudence nodded, her nostrils filled with the familiar scent of disinfectant, which the hospital used to mask the stench of blood and vomit. She joined the queue and waited calmly for her turn, then took a seat, knowing it would be a while before they got to her. She wished she'd thought to bring her Kindle.

Zoe sat beside her, still tapping away on her phone. Was it Nathan she was talking to? Prudence didn't think so. He had lectures, so he would be too busy to reply. She tried to get a look over Zoe's shoulder, but the font was too small for her to read without her glasses.

Zoe shot her a look. "Any idea how long we'll be?"

"Could be hours," Prudence said with a sigh. "There's a bus stop outside if you want to head home."

"Nah, I'll wait with you," Zoe said. "Besides, if they keep us waiting much longer I'll be ready to give birth."

Prudence raised an eyebrow. She couldn't remember the last time Zoe had cracked a joke.

"Prudence Ahern?" An agency nurse waved her into a cubicle.

"Wait here, please. The doctor will be with you shortly."

"Which one?" Prudence asked.

"I'm sorry?"

"I used to work here, so I might know the doctor."

"Oh, right." The nurse couldn't have looked less interested. Prudence clammed up and let her finish her assessment in peace.

She didn't know the doctor, as it turned out. He looked around Nathan's age and twice as spotty. He checked her notes with a puzzled expression.

"It says here you got an electric shock from a lawnmower. What happened? Was the grass wet?"

Prudence frowned. "No, I don't think so."

"How does the arm feel now?"

"Better," she admitted. "I'm starting to feel it again now. It's just a bit sore."

She waited while he listened to her heart. The stethoscope felt like ice on her chest.

"You should rub it on your sleeve first," she told him.

He looked at her oddly. "Well, your heart sounds okay. Any headaches?"

"A little."

"Can you raise your arm?"

She tried and, to her relief, she found she could.

"Good. I'd advise you to take it easy for the rest of the day. Plenty of fluids."

Prudence nodded.

"And don't use that dodgy mower again. This could have been very serious indeed. It's a good thing your daughter was there to take care of you."

"Oh, she's not my ..."

The doctor had already turned his attention to someone else and Prudence was just staring at his back now.

"You might want to work on your bedside manner," she said under her breath.

She rose to her feet. She still felt a little jittery, but she wasn't going to die. Not today, anyway. She walked back out to the waiting room, where Zoe sat texting under a sign expressly forbidding mobile phones.

"Are they going to keep you in?"

"No. I can go home now."

"Oh. Okay."

A look flashed across Zoe's face. Was that annoyance? Prudence couldn't tell. Then Zoe smiled brightly. "Right, I'll ring Nathan and see if he can pick us up."

Nathan was going to be a while, so they headed to the

coffee shop to wait. Prudence paid for their lattes and muffins and Zoe didn't object. They found a quiet corner and sat down.

"Tell me, when did you first realise you were pregnant?" Prudence asked, as she bit into her muffin. "With Nathan, it was my tastebuds that tipped me off. I couldn't drink tea for the whole nine months."

Zoe looked thoughtful. "One of my housemates smoked a lot of weed. I didn't mind it at first but then the smell seemed unbearably sweet. It made me want to puke. That was when Nathan asked if I was pregnant. It sounds stupid, but I seriously hadn't considered it before. I never had any plans to become a mum. I've always been so focused on my career."

Prudence swallowed the rest of her muffin. She wanted to ask Zoe about her previous boyfriends, but she wasn't sure how to phrase it without sounding nosey.

"Was it hard moving away from home?" she asked instead.

Zoe frowned. "In what way?"

"You know, leaving your family. Your ... friends."

She examined her nails. "I didn't really have many friends. Oh, look, there's Nathan!"

It was. Zoe waved, and he walked into the coffee shop.

"Mum! What the hell happened? Jon said you'd been electrocuted."

"I had an accident with the lawnmower," she told him. "But I'm alright now."

"You look as white as a sheet."

"Yeah, I think you and Zoe had better take care of dinner tonight. And the dishes. Maybe put a load of washing on too. I'm much too weak."

Nathan smiled. "Don't push your luck."

15

PRUDENCE

"The lawnmower shouldn't give you electric shocks if it's been properly maintained," said the woman at the lawnmower company.

"It has. My son takes good care of it."

"Well, if he takes good care of it, it should still be working."

"I'm telling you it gave me a bloody big electric shock."

She heard a rustling sound, like the woman was consulting a guidebook.

"As your lawnmower is out of warranty there's not much we can do for you. However, if you would like to bring it up to our headquarters we'll take a look."

"And where's that?"

"We're based in Sheffield. I can send you the address."

"Don't bother. I'm not driving all the way up there. I suggest you send someone to collect it. There is a public safety case to answer here. I could have been killed. I really think your product should be recalled."

More rustling sounds.

"Madam, if you are going to threaten me, then I will have to end the call."

"I'm not threatening you. I'm stating a fact."

"May I remind you that this call is being recorded?"

"Good. You need to have this on record. You need to recall your product."

"DON'T TOUCH THE MOWER AGAIN," Nathan warned her after she hung up. "If they're not going to replace it, we might as well take it to the tip."

"Hmm." Prudence was miffed. It seemed like no one was willing to take responsibility for their mistakes anymore. Still, she'd leave it for now and pick up a new one in the sales.

ZOE AND NATHAN were spending that weekend at Alana's. Prudence was glad Nathan was taking time off. He'd been working so hard lately, it seemed like he rarely had a break. All the same, the minute they drove off she was left with crushing silence. When she was working, she would have relished a weekend all to herself but now the hours stretched out ahead of her and she just couldn't get into anything. She took out her notebook, where she had written a long list of all the things she wanted to do, but none of them inspired her so she took to her bed and watched back-to-back episodes of *Strictly Come Dancing*.

Heidi was also busy that weekend – she'd gone to see her sister in Crewe. Prudence had other friends, of course she did. But Caroline was busy with her family and Jackie was one of those people who was great fun in a group but a bit much on their own, and Prudence didn't particularly feel like going out dancing till two in the morning or drinking a yard of ale. Honestly, she was much more content to stay home and watch TV with a tube of Pringles for company.

Nathan and Zoe returned home Sunday afternoon.

"How was Alana?" Prudence asked.

"Not much of a cook," Nathan said. "Her fridge was full of wine and we ate takeaway pizza for breakfast, lunch and dinner. Mum, she's done up a nursery in her spare room."

"Has she?" Prudence said. That was one of the jobs on her list.

"She's gone all out and painted the room pink. There are pink frilly curtains and a little pink rocking horse. It's a little nauseating. She's got a cot and a changing table and everything in there. Quite over the top, considering we'll only be visiting about once a month."

Prudence smiled. "Sounds like someone's excited. Actually, I was thinking of starting on our nursery this week."

She hadn't been but now she felt like she ought to.

"Great, Mum, just do me a favour and don't paint it pink."

"What colour would you like? I was thinking maybe yellow or green?"

Nathan gave her an impish grin. "Paint it blue."

Nathan was right; it didn't matter if the baby was a girl, blue was a nice colour. And if she did turn out to be a girly girl, they could always add in some more feminine features. She bought a rocking chair for Zoe to sit in when she was feeding the baby. She recalled how many hours she'd spent sitting around with Nathan. Comfort was important. She didn't have room for a changing table, so she chose a colourful changing mat and a large cabinet she could put on the wall. The cabinet was a good size and ought to be big enough for all the baby's things.

"You expecting?" said the man at the checkout when she went to pay.

He gestured to all the baby stuff in her trolley and Prudence burst out laughing. "Oh no, all this is for my grand-daughter."

At least, I hope it is.

She had already bought yellow bedding for the cot and had a little Moses basket Jackie had given her, so the room wouldn't be totally blue. Perhaps she could put in yellow curtains for contrast.

Prudence liked a project. She put on her old jumpsuit, a relic from the 1980s when this sort of thing had last been in fashion. Funny enough, she'd seen one of Nathan's friends wearing one in Morrisons, so that just went to show how everything came back in. She set her old portable radio down in one corner and tuned to Carillion Radio.

The walls took longer than she thought. She painted the ceiling white, because it looked a little gloomy. She was up and down the ladder constantly. Zoe brought her cups of tea throughout the day, which she was grateful for, although she drank the first cup with caution, paranoid in case Zoe had laced it with laxatives or something.

"You've done such an amazing job!" Zoe gushed, when Prudence had finished painting.

"It's amazing, Mum!" Nathan agreed. "You should start your own painting and decorating company."

"Oh, I don't know about that," Prudence said with a smile. She was pleased, though. The colour was bright and cheer-ful, and she'd applied it evenly. No big splotches or drips anywhere to be seen.

She gave the paint a day to dry before she moved the furniture back in. She placed the cot on the right and the big cabinet on the left, with the rocking chair by the window. Zoe had a meeting with her tutor that morning, but when she came home for lunch she brought Prudence a cherry bakewell.

"I thought you might be hungry after all your hard work. Wow, it all looks amazing. I really like the blue."

Prudence nodded. "Me, too."

She went and washed her hands, then returned and sat down in the rocking chair to enjoy the view. It still whiffed a bit of paint, but that would go. There was a nice view of the garden from here. As she bit into her cake, the phone rang. She jumped up from her seat. As she stood, the cabinet fell off the wall, narrowly missing her as it crashed to the ground.

Prudence stared at it, her heart beating fast. Another couple of inches and it would have hit her. All at once, Zoe was in the doorway. Her face was red with anger.

"Oh my god, that's so dangerous! What if the baby had been sitting there? You could have killed it."

Prudence shook her head. "I screwed it tight to the wall, I swear! I ... I don't know what happened."

They both stared at the mess. The cabinet had a glass front, which had shattered all over the floor.

Prudence could barely breathe.

"I screwed it to the wall," she repeated. She thought fast. She had only left the room briefly to wash her hands. Had Zoe snuck in and loosened the screws? It seemed unlikely, and yet Prudence couldn't understand how else it had happened.

Zoe stomped back to her room, while Prudence bent down to examine the damage. She was going to have to get another door for the front. She'd get a wooden one, that would be safer. And this time she was going to make sure it was securely attached, even if it meant adding in another row of screws.

She cleared away all the glass, then started to head downstairs. She wasn't sure what made her turn and look back, but when she did she saw that the door to Nathan and Zoe's room was ajar. Zoe was spying on her; she could sense it.

Her heart pumped a little faster. Another day, another accident. But would Zoe really sabotage her own child's nursery? It didn't make sense. As she watched, the door slowly closed and Prudence felt more bewildered than ever. *What the hell was going on?* Her imagination was out of control and yet she couldn't shift the feeling that Zoe wanted to get rid of her.

16

ZOE

From: Zoe Nithercott <Zoe.Nithercott@lbro.ac.uk>
To: Ted Nithercott <Edward.Nithercott@gmail.com>
Subject: Sorry

Dad,

Sorry I ghosted you. I didn't mean to, I just haven't been in the mood to write. I've been feeling totally shit about the baby situation. The scan showed it's a girl but the Prune said the scan might be wrong so now I don't know what to think. I'm still hoping it's a boy but I know I'm probably kidding myself.

I had a look at the website. There were so many children on there. It made me want to vomit. All their pictures are displayed with names and ages. I can't stand looking at them. Each one represents a little soul. What are people supposed to do, just pick out the one they want, based on looks?

And what about the prospective parents? How can you tell if someone will be any good just by looking at their picture or reading their CV? I mean, I know the social are supposed to vet them but what do they really know about these people? Anything could happen behind closed doors.

For now, it's easier to stick my head in the sand. I'll wait until the baby is born, then I'll know for sure. Until then, I've got Nathan working every shift he can. His friend Bradley was ill with the flu for a couple of weeks so he'll make almost double this month. It all helps.

I had a job interview for a cashier at a building society last week. It sounded quite promising on the phone but as soon as they saw my bump I knew I was wasting my time. No one wants to employ a pregnant woman. If it comes to it, I can sell Nathan's car and whatever bric-a-brac we can get from the Prune. In the meantime, I'm applying for a bunch of credit cards.

Zoe xxx

PS - Miss you loads!

17

"Who are you texting?" Prudence asked, as Zoe once again reached for her phone.

"Just my mum."

Bullshit, Prudence thought. No teenager talked to their mum that much. More likely, she was talking to boys. Or maybe just one boy. For her son's sake, she hoped it was Nathan.

Zoe had taken over the kitchen table, dirty dishes piled up around her. She must have used a different mug every time she made herself a cup of tea and she was constantly eating. Her pregnancy had made her ravenous. Every time Prudence saw her she was shovelling cereal into her mouth or biting into a sandwich. To begin with, Prudence would pick up her plates and mugs and stick them in the dishwasher to demonstrate where they should go, but Zoe never seemed to take the hint so Prudence stopped clearing up after her, even though the mess irritated her beyond belief.

Then, ten minutes before Nathan was due home, Zoe would suddenly jump up and shove everything in the dishwasher. Sometimes, she even stuck an easy-bake baguette in the oven so that by the time Nathan arrived the house was filled with the delicious aroma of baking bread.

ONE EVENING, Nathan and Zoe were sitting in the lounge after dinner.

"Let's hope it doesn't come to that," she heard Nathan say as she walked in.

"What's that?" she asked.

But Nathan just shot her a look. "We were talking about Zoe's coursework," he said. "She doesn't know if she's going to be able to complete the year before the baby comes."

"I'm sure I can," Zoe said hurriedly.

"Just as long as you're not putting yourself under too much pressure," Prudence said. "Your health comes first. You can always catch up on any work you miss later. You have a valid excuse."

Zoe nodded absently, but she still looked a little troubled.

They all fell silent, and Zoe and Nathan became focused on an old episode of *The Apprentice*. Prudence was not a fan of the show but she knew Zoe loved Sir Alan Sugar.

She settled in her armchair and watched her son. He had one hand draped protectively around Zoe's shoulder. They looked so natural together, like they belonged. She and Nathan almost never spent any time together anymore because Zoe was always there. There had been a time when he would sit and watch *Strictly* with her on a Saturday night, but now he and Zoe watched *Dragon's Den* and she had to record *Strictly* and watch it on Sunday morning, when they were both in bed. But it wasn't the same watching it on her own. She needed someone to gossip with, someone who would *ooh* and *aah* as she exclaimed about the dresses. Even though it wasn't exactly Nathan's cup of tea, he had always made her laugh with his wisecracks about the contestants.

. . .

"Haven't seen much of Nathan lately," Heidi commented on Friday afternoon, as the two of them sipped lattes in the health club after Zumba.

"I hardly see him myself. He's been working really long hours," Prudence said, swirling the foam with her spoon. "I'm concerned that he's letting his uni work slip. He's so focused on earning money so that he and Zoe can get their own place."

"What's the rush? Are you planning to turf them out?"

"Hardly."

"Does Nathan know that?"

"He ought to."

"What about Zoe?"

Prudence sighed. "I've no idea what Zoe is thinking. She barely even looks at me most of the time."

"I expect she's tired. It can't be long now."

"She's got a few more weeks yet, but then first babies are usually late, so who knows?"

"Well, it sounds to me like you need to talk to Nathan," Heidi said calmly. "Let him know that there's no rush for them to move out."

"He does know," Prudence told her. But perhaps she would talk to him, just in case.

She cornered Nathan that evening after dinner. "You're working so hard. I just don't understand why you would risk your uni work this way. There's no rush for you and Zoe to move out. You can stay here as long as you like. You do know that, don't you?"

"Of course, Mum."

Was it her imagination or was his smile forced?

"Alternatively, why don't you put yourselves down for a council house? It'd be a lot cheaper than renting privately. You might have to wait a bit, but it would be better in the long run."

"Yeah, maybe."

He was looking right at her and nodding his head, but she had the feeling that he wasn't listening to a word she was saying.

The phone rang. It was Alana.

"Oh, hi, Prudence. I was just wondering how Zoe's doing? She was supposed to ring at five. I suppose she must have forgotten."

"Zoe seems fine, Alana. How are you doing?"

"Excited and anxious," Alana admitted. "I feel bad that I'm so far away when she needs me."

"Don't worry, I'm a nurse. She couldn't be in safer hands."

"That's true, I just worry about her, you know? Zoe lives in a bit of a fantasy world, and I just worry that the pregnancy might tip her over the edge."

"In what way?"

"I don't know exactly. Just all those hormones buzzing around. I'm sure she's fine. Forget I said anything."

Zoe was approaching. "Is that my mum?"

Prudence nodded. "Nice talking to you, Alana. I'll put Zoe on."

Zoe gave her a look, so she walked into the kitchen and made herself a cup of tea, but she wished she could have talked to Alana a little longer. She felt like she'd been about to open up about something. Something that might have explained more about Zoe.

Zoe and Nathan went up to bed early, and Prudence resigned herself to a night alone on the sofa, but at a quarter to midnight she heard footsteps on the stairs. She looked up and saw Nathan.

"Can't sleep?" she asked.

"I wanted to ask you something."

She patted the sofa next to her and he sat down.

"Mum, I was wondering if I could have Granny's ring? I want to propose to Zoe, and I can't afford a new one, but I thought maybe I could give her Granny's? Antiques are all the rage."

Prudence swallowed hard. *You don't even know if it's your baby*, she wanted to scream.

Instead she said: "It might be better to wait until the baby is born."

"Why?"

"You don't want to put Zoe under any pressure. She's heavily pregnant now. She's bound to be a bit emotional."

"You think she'll say no?"

"No, I just don't think you should rush into it."

Nathan rubbed his eyes and laughed. "Don't you think that ship's already sailed?"

On Monday morning, Prudence returned from Morrisons to find Heidi sitting at the kitchen table, having a cosy cup of tea with Zoe. She wasn't sure why, but it irked her to see her best friend being so chummy with her son's girlfriend.

She set her bags down on the counter and put the ice-cream straight into the freezer. The rest could wait.

"Zoe was just telling me about her latest cravings," Heidi said.

"Oh, yeah?" Prudence asked.

"You're going to be disgusted," Zoe warned her.

"Go on."

"Strawberry and tuna," Zoe said with a groan.

"Oh god, you aren't serious?"

"I am. I ate a whole bowl of it earlier."

Prudence forced a laugh. "That sounds pretty dire."

"Well, got to love you and leave you," Heidi said, getting to her feet.

Prudence was disappointed. With Heidi there, Zoe was actually acting like a human being. She wanted to get more out of her.

"Wait, one more cup of tea," she begged.

Heidi must have caught the desperation in her eyes. "Oh, alright then. Just the one."

Prudence switched on the kettle. "I saw Charlie in Morrisons this morning," she said.

Zoe and Heidi both looked at her.

"I hope you didn't take him back," Zoe said in disgust.

"No, I hid in the cheese aisle," she admitted. She had been tempted to go up and talk to him, but then she saw that he was with another woman and lost her nerve. Charlie had clearly moved on.

"He wasn't the man for you. When you meet the right man, you just know," Zoe said with authority.

"How did you know Nathan was the one?" Heidi asked.

"There was something in his eyes. I could tell he was kind and thoughtful the first time I saw him and when he looks at me, it's like he sees something no one else does."

She had that part right.

"So he's different to your other boyfriends?" Prudence asked, pouring fresh tea into the pot.

Heidi gave her a look.

"I haven't had any other boyfriends," Zoe said, folding her arms.

"I could have sworn your mother mentioned—"

"She just meant the neighbourhood kids. Most of them were boys."

Heidi rose abruptly. "Sorry, chaps, I've just noticed the time. I'm supposed to be meeting a friend for tennis."

"Okay, have a nice game," Prudence called. She was still looking at Zoe, and was fairly sure she was lying.

"Right, well, I'm going to take a bath," Zoe said, clambering to her feet. Getting up seemed to take quite an effort now she was so big, and Prudence hoped she'd be able to hoist herself out of the bath. Zoe turned and looked at Prudence.

"Can I ask you something?"

"Of course! Anything."

"How will I know when I'm in labour?"

"Oh, you'll know."

Zoe gripped the table. Her face contorted, then she relaxed again. Prudence waited for the moment to pass.

"Feeling better?"

Zoe nodded. "What do I do now?"

"Just carry on as normal and see if it happens again. You've got your bag packed, haven't you?"

"It's been packed for over a month."

"Good girl. Now why don't you take that bath or watch a bit of TV or something, whatever takes your mind off it."

Prudence threw the cups into the dishwasher, barely caring where they went. She found Zoe in the lounge, rocking back and forth on the sofa.

"Another pain?"

Zoe couldn't speak.

Prudence sat close and waited. "How long have you been getting the pains, Zoe?"

"On and off all morning."

"They seem fairly regular now. I think this could be it. We should call your midwife. And Nathan."

"Nathan first," Zoe said through her teeth.

"Okay, I'll call him now. You get on to your midwife."

A shiver of excitement ran through her as she picked up the phone to call her son. He'd be in a lecture now. She hoped he had his phone on or she'd have to go down there and get him.

Nathan answered on the third ring.

"Zoe's gone into labour," she told him. "Can you get someone to drive you to the hospital?"

Zoe looked alarmed. "No, tell him to come here! We need to go together."

Prudence shook her head. "I really think we should get you to the hospital. I've been timing your contractions. They're only five minutes apart."

"Shit!"

"It's okay. There's still plenty of time."

"I'm not going without Nathan!" Zoe wailed.

"I'm on my way!" Nathan said and hung up.

Prudence turned to Zoe. "Let's wait for him in the car then. Do you want me to get your bag?"

"No, I'll get it."

She watched with concern as Zoe climbed the stairs. Why wouldn't she accept her help? This was hardly the time to fight.

She picked up the phone and called Alana. She didn't know why she hadn't thought to before. A girl needed her mother. And god knows Alana must have been waiting for her call.

"Alana, this is Prudence."

"Is Zoe in labour?"

"I think she is."

"I can't believe it! My baby's having a baby!"

"I know!"

"I was supposed to be going to a conference this afternoon. I'd better cancel it. And I had a delivery coming ..."

Prudence smiled.

"Alana, we're going to Leicester General. We'll meet you there."

"Tell Zoe to hang on and wait for me."

"I don't think she can hang on."

"You will stay with her, won't you?"

"Of course, I will. I'm going to let you go now. You've got a long drive ahead of you."

Zoe huffed back down the stairs, dragging a brown holdall.

"Here, let me take that," Prudence said. "You need to save your energy."

Before she could say anything else, Zoe's face contorted again. She was in the grip of another powerful contraction. They were getting so close now, Prudence was concerned she'd have the baby in the car.

"I rang your mum. She's on her way," she told her soothingly.

"Leave me alone," Zoe said, shoving her away. Prudence was shocked. She was only trying to help.

"Honey, I'm home!" Nathan called.

Prudence sighed with relief.

Zoe rushed to the door and they embraced each other, then Zoe's water broke all over his shoes.

"Right then," Prudence said. "We need to go."

THE MIDWIFE AGREED with Prudence's assessment that Zoe needed to go straight to her room. Zoe was planning to give birth in one of the midwife-led birthing suites. Prudence had never been in there before, so she was curious to see it. The room had a very relaxed, homely feel and was stocked with a couple of large birthing balls and some comfortable mats to lie on.

Nathan removed a speaker from Zoe's bag and set up the music she planned to give birth to. He had personally spent hours compiling the playlist.

"It looks really relaxing," she told Zoe, who was already tensing up for her next contraction.

"Nathan!" she nudged her son. "Stop mucking about with the music and hold her hand!"

"Just a minute!"

He pressed play and soft, soothing music filled the room. Zoe visibly relaxed, despite her pain.

"Right, well, I'm going to leave you two alone now," Prudence said, wanting to give Zoe some privacy. "But I'll be right outside if you need me."

She walked out into the waiting room and wondered what she should do with herself. She felt like pacing the corridors, like one of those dads in old black and white films. She wondered about popping down to the coffee shop to get some refreshments. She would probably be waiting a while and there wasn't much on this floor besides a machine that sold really bad coffee. She rummaged in her handbag for her purse, but then she changed her mind. She had promised Alana she would stay with Zoe. She should wait until she arrived.

She heard Zoe's screams from the waiting room. There had been no time to give her any pain relief. It seemed like the baby was in a rush to be born.

"The baby's coming now," someone said. "Nice big push, Zoe."

She heard another scream followed by a big thud. She jumped to her feet.

"What's happening?"

The student midwife came to the door. "It's okay, this happens sometimes. He'll be alright."

"Nathan?"

"He just fainted."

"Oh my god."

"He'll be okay."

The other midwife came to the door. "Quick, Zoe wants you to come in."

Prudence looked around. "It shouldn't be me, it should be her mother."

"She's not here. You are."

18

PRUDENCE

Prudence followed the midwife into the delivery room. Nathan lay prone on the floor. There was a young nurse taking care of him. They'd propped a pillow under his head and turned him on his side. His eyes flickered as she passed and for a moment she was tempted to go to him instead of Zoe, but then Zoe gave such a shriek of pain that she rushed to her side.

"I'm here, Zoe. It's okay."

Zoe gave a throaty grunt as she took her hand.

The midwife smiled. "Come on, Zoe. The baby's nearly here. One big push."

Zoe tucked her chin to her chest and bore down with all her might. Prudence did her best to grip her hand, although her palms were slick with sweat.

"You can do it, Zoe!" she whispered.

Zoe squirmed and contorted, then all at once she collapsed back against the pillows. Prudence glanced down at the midwife, who held up the baby.

There was no sound. The nurse suctioned the baby's nose

and it let out an earth-shattering wail. Prudence let out all the breath she'd been holding.

"Well done, Zoe," she said. "You're a mum."

"Congratulations," the midwife added. "You've got a beautiful baby girl."

Zoe began to sob uncontrollably. Her shoulders shook and tears streamed down her face.

"Your baby's fine," the midwife assured her, but Zoe kept on crying. Prudence handed her a glass of water.

"Here, drink this."

Zoe drank the water, but she continued to sob between gulps.

Prudence looked over at Nathan. He was sitting up now, but still a little pale. He looked over at the baby. "She's beautiful," he told Zoe. "Just like you."

The midwife finished wiping the baby down and laid her on Zoe's chest, but she was too overwrought to take her, so she passed her to Prudence.

"Just take her."

Prudence smiled down at the little bundle in her arms. She looked just like Nathan when he was born. Same puckered lips and long wispy eyelashes. Her heart swelled with joy.

"Can I have a hold?" Nathan asked.

"Yes, of course." She carried the baby across the room to Nathan, who held her close to his chest.

"We've chosen the name Bonnie," he told her. "After Gran."

Tears welled in Prudence's eyes. Her mother would have been so proud.

She stepped out of the room to allow Zoe some privacy while she delivered the placenta.

Should she ring Alana? she wondered. She was probably desperate for news but Prudence didn't want her to veer off the road. She decided it would be best to wait until she arrived.

She waited until the nursing team had finished with Zoe, then went back in. Zoe was looking a little better. She'd stopped crying and was sitting up in bed.

"What do you think, Zoe? Are you ready to meet your daughter?"

Zoe mumbled something. She looked afraid, which seemed impossible, because who could be afraid of a sweet little newborn? Nathan crossed the room and placed Bonnie gently in her arms.

"Shall I take a picture of the three of you?" Prudence offered, pulling out her phone.

She took a couple, keen to capture the moment. She planned to frame it and give it to them as a present. These moments were so precious and they went by so quickly. It was important to hold on to them as best you could.

Zoe continued to hold the baby, gazing at her as if trying to memorise every detail. Prudence remembered how she had looked at Nathan when he was born. It had been love at first sight. She recalled how she had counted every finger, every toe, and had been delighted it was all there. When the midwife confirmed both his testicles had dropped, she had wept with joy.

"I'm here."

Alana strode into the room, dressed in a slightly crumpled linen suit. Her hair was pulled up into an elegant bun, with a few tendrils hanging loose.

"Hello, gorgeous!" She swept Bonnie up in her arms and gazed adoringly at her face. "She's perfect," she breathed. "Absolutely perfect!"

"Isn't she?" Prudence agreed. She glanced at Zoe, but she gave no reaction.

"Definitely a girl," Alana said, peering under the towel.

"She is," Nathan said, moving towards her.

Alana gazed into the baby's eyes. She rocked her in her arms and sung her a lullaby. Then she walked over to the window with her and pointed out the sky and the trees and the birds in the distance.

"I have so much to teach you," she told her. "You are going to be a big deal one day, a really big deal. Oh look, you can see my car in the car park. It's the pink shiny one. Do you like it? I bet you do, don't you?"

She was being a baby hog, not that Prudence could blame her. She ached to hold Bonnie again herself. She couldn't believe how much she looked like Nathan. Bonnie was starting to stir now. She gave a little snuffle and screwed up her eyes. Here we go, thought Prudence, as she produced a small wail.

"Shh, shh," Alana soothed her, holding her close to her chest.

Prudence took a step forward. "I think she needs to go back to Zoe now. She hasn't had much chance to feed."

Alana bit her lip and handed the baby back to her daughter. Zoe held her stiffly. She looked unnatural, Prudence thought. She held Bonnie like she was holding a water bottle. But it would come. She would soon learn.

"Oh, I have presents!" Alana said, with a snap of her fingers. She darted from the room.

Zoe held Bonnie to her breast and Prudence resisted the urge to correct her position. Zoe was nervous enough as it was; she didn't want to destroy her confidence.

"Perhaps you'd like a pillow under your elbow?" she suggested instead. She motioned to Nathan to fetch one.

With the pillow in place, Bonnie started to suckle. Nathan settled himself on the chair beside the bed.

"I feel like such an idiot for passing out like that," he said sheepishly.

"You won't be the last," Prudence told him fondly. At least he'd been willing to attend the birth. His own father hadn't come to see him until his second day in hospital. Not that she had needed him. She hadn't needed anybody. It would have been nice, though, to have a supportive partner to hold her hand. She had felt his absence keenly those first few days. She couldn't believe he really didn't want to be in their lives.

Alana returned ten minutes later with a huge bag full of girls' clothes, all of them in varying shades of pink and purple.

"She must have fed by now," she told Zoe.

Zoe didn't object so Alana took Bonnie and changed her from her plain Babygro into a flouncy pink dress.

The midwife looked into the room. "How are you doing?" she asked Zoe. "Oh, doesn't she look scrumptious?" she said, looking at Bonnie.

Alana glowed at the praise.

"Ah, you must be Zoe's mum. She's going to need lots of help from you over the next few days."

"Yes, of course," Alana said.

"Now, it's nearly the end of visiting time so I need you all to say your goodbyes and let Zoe and little one get some rest."

Prudence picked up her bag. She'd been expecting this anyway.

The midwife smiled kindly at Zoe. "My colleague will be in soon to do your stitches, okay, my love?"

Prudence tensed involuntarily, but Zoe seemed to take this in her stride.

"I'd like to stay with my daughter until your colleague arrives," Alana said.

"Alright then. It'll only be about ten minutes or so."

Nathan and Zoe exchanged pointed looks, but Prudence wasn't sure what they were about.

"I'll finish that thing we agreed on," Nathan said in Zoe's

ear as he left. Zoe glanced over at Alana, who had a quizzical look on her face. Whatever they were talking about, she wasn't in on it.

Prudence and Nathan walked out to the car, and she showed him the picture she'd taken on her phone. It was only then she noticed how blank the expression on Zoe's face was.

19
___
ZOE

From: Zoe Nithercott <Zoe.Nithercott@lbro.ac.uk>
To: Ted Nithercott <Edward.Nithercott@gmail.com>
Subject: You're a grandad!

Dad,

The baby is here and surprise, surprise, it's a girl. We've called her Bonnie. If she'd been a boy, I was going to name him Ted after you. She doesn't sleep much, she mostly cries, but that's probably my fault. I think she can sense I'm not a proper mum. I'm too young, too selfish. I don't think I was meant to be a mum. All the other mums look like they know what they're doing. They all smile like Mother Teresa and tell you that of course they're tired but their baby is the best thing that ever happened to them, whereas for me, it's the worst.

It's not Bonnie's fault. Don't hold it against her. But I wish I could wind back time to before she ever existed. I was so nervous when I first started uni. I rang Mum that first night and begged her to come and get me. But she told me to give it a week and I'm so glad I did, because I met Nathan and he was everything I didn't know I needed. I never met a man like him before. I never knew anyone could be so loving and caring, whilst also being funny and hot and just, supportive in every way. I thought I knew everything there was to know about love – after all, didn't I empty the shelves of YA romance books at the library every week? But Nathan wasn't like any of those boys. He wasn't like anyone I'd ever known. We were so happy before I found out about Bonnie, and now I have this feeling of panic like I'm stuck on the motorway with no service stations and no exit and any minute I just know I'm going to crash.

I know what you're thinking. There are alternatives. But it's not as easy as all that. I couldn't go through with the adoption. I couldn't even make the call. There was no way of knowing if the person I picked would be the right one. And then there was Nathan to think about. He loves Bonnie and he deserves to be a dad. He's really good at it too; he seems to understand instinctively what she wants. It's like he knows which cry means she's hungry and which one means she just needs a cuddle. He's like that with me too. He gets me the way no one else ever has.

But I can't sit around here feeling sorry for myself, so here's the latest plan: I'm going to take legal action. Nathan can help me with that. We can cut the problem off at the source. And if that doesn't work, then I'll have to go with the more drastic option. It scares the shit out of me, but I'm prepared to do whatever it takes to survive.

I'm so tired, Dad. My body feels like it's covered with invisible bruises and I don't know if they're ever going to heal. No one tells you how much giving birth hurts and they all tell you that you'll forget about it once it's over but it's all a big lie. It was hideous. Nathan thought so too. He passed out and I had to go through it all without him. He's really sorry though. He told me if he could have had the baby for me, he would have. I had to forgive him when he said that.

I'm feeling really low now, so if you still care even a little bit, then I know you'll fix this mess for me. I'm running out of ideas and I'm really scared in case things don't go my way. I just need you to make it right. I know I'm all grown up now and I should stand on my own two feet, but right now I really need my dad.

Zoe xxx

20

PRUDENCE

Nathan tossed the old nappy into the bin. Bonnie gazed up him as he changed her into a fresh one. It was much too soon for her to be smiling and yet she had a very content look on her face, close to adoration.

"I think she's going to be a daddy's girl," Prudence said with a grin.

"I just wish I had more time with her," he said.

"Well, why don't you take some time off work? You've been doing so many shifts lately. Surely you can afford to take a break?"

Nathan frowned and she got the distinct feeling there was something he wasn't telling her. She waited, but he merely plonked Bonnie into her arms and picked up his backpack.

"Sorry, Mum. I've got to get going."

"Alright then, but think about what I said. You really don't need to work so many hours. Bonnie will only be little for a very short time. You should make the most of her."

He nodded, but his face remained clouded, and she wondered if he was worried about Zoe. Perhaps he thought he had to do the work of two people because she wasn't coping too well. Zoe had struggled to breastfeed and seemed relieved when the midwife suggested she switch to bottle feeding after a couple of days. Since then, Prudence had been the one to give Bonnie most of her feeds. She didn't intend to take over, it was just that Zoe had yet to find her mojo.

Occasionally, she thought about contacting Nathan's dad, to let him know that he was a granddad. But he hadn't been interested in becoming a father, so why should this be any different? Knowing him, he would probably question whether the baby was really Nathan's. There was no more doubt in her own mind, though. Bonnie was so obviously Nathan's child that she'd taken the paternity test she had bought and dumped it in the outside bin.

THE DAYS TURNED into weeks and still Zoe couldn't seem to kick her tiredness. Prudence was increasingly concerned and suspected Zoe might have postnatal depression. Sally the midwife popped in at the beginning of the third week, but suddenly Zoe was all smiles. She picked Bonnie up for the first time that day and batted back all of Sally's questions like a pro. It was astounding to watch, and Prudence began to wonder if she'd been worrying for nothing, but as soon as Sally left, Zoe dumped Bonnie in Prudence's arms and retreated to her room, where she remained for the rest of the day. Prudence thought about calling Sally back, but it was nearly the weekend and Alana was due to visit. If anyone could get through to Zoe, it would be her mum.

Alana arrived in a different car this time, a dark blue BMW that looked like it had come straight from the show-room. She walked up the drive, carrying two large bags, which she set down in the kitchen.

"Mum, we do have food in the fridge," Zoe grumbled, as her mother pulled out a round of camembert with caramelised onions and fancy ham from the delicatessen. In her other bag were artisan loaves and French wine.

"That's what mums do, feed people," Alana said fondly. She poured Zoe a glass of wine and pushed it towards her. "Since you're not breastfeeding."

She poured a glass for Prudence too. She always seemed to take this role, even though it wasn't her house. Prudence didn't mind a bit. She understood it was just what Alana did. Some people were natural hosts.

Prudence sipped her wine slowly. She didn't want to be a killjoy, but one of them needed to remain sober in order to care for Bonnie.

"Now, where's my granddaughter?" Alana asked.

"She's taking a nap in the nursery," Zoe said.

"I'll just take a little peek. I won't wake her, I promise."

Prudence suddenly felt tired. She knew Alana was family, but she wasn't sure she was up to socialising. All she really wanted to do was sleep, but she didn't want to appear rude.

A few minutes later, Alana came back downstairs. "I swear she's grown already."

"I think you're right," Prudence agreed. Already, Bonnie's newborn outfits were getting a little small.

A few minutes later, Bonnie woke up, so Alana gave her her bottle whilst regaling them all with more stories of Zoe's childhood. Prudence tried to listen, but her eyes were closing. Alana's voice had a hypnotic quality and she could barely stay awake.

When she opened her eyes, she realised Alana was still talking:

"... the time Zoe climbed out of her bedroom window to meet up with this boy she'd met at the market. The first I knew of it was when the chip pan caught fire and I had to call out the fire brigade. When Zoe didn't appear, they went up to her room convinced she'd been overcome with fumes, but no, she was just parked in some boy's car, being a typical teenager."

Zoe laughed loudly but Prudence blinked with confusion. She was certain she'd heard this story before, but the details were different. Zoe didn't correct her, though. It was all rather odd. She wished Nathan was there – he would remember – but he was out working again.

Alana stayed late into the night and Prudence remained awake with the aid of caffeine. Zoe seemed perked up by her company. Whenever Alana told a joke, Zoe laughed loudest of all. Perhaps this was what she'd been missing, a bit of fun, Prudence thought. But when she looked at Zoe closely, she saw there was something frenzied about her.

Later, Alana took Prudence to one side. "I wanted to thank you for everything you've done for Zoe."

Prudence leaned back against the fridge. "It's nothing. I love being a grandmother. Well, you know. It's the most amazing feeling in the world. Zoe is welcome to stay as long as she wants, but to be honest, I am a little worried about her. I mean I know she's young and it's all a little daunting, but she seems a little ... absent, emotionally. Do you think she's alright?"

Alana sighed. "Perhaps she could use a change of scenery? I'm due a few days' leave. I was planning to take the Eurostar to Paris but perhaps Zoe and Bonnie should come home for a bit instead."

"Well, that might help," Prudence said, but she wasn't so sure. She had Bonnie in a routine now, and she knew what she was doing. Not to suggest that Alana couldn't do just as good a job, but she was clearly a career woman, and a bit of a party girl, judging by the amount of alcohol she consumed. Not that she ever seemed particularly drunk.

"I think that would be good, but we are just getting Bonnie into a routine, so maybe we should wait a few weeks?"

Alana frowned. Perhaps she had expected Prudence to jump at the chance, then she nodded and topped up their glasses.

"Well, the offer's there, any time. Just give me a call."

"Thank you," said Prudence. "I will."

THAT NIGHT, after Alana left, Prudence tiptoed into the nursery to check on Bonnie. She drew in her breath as she spotted a figure standing over the crib. A light shone in through the window – she must have forgotten to close the curtains, and she could clearly see Zoe's face as she stared down at the sleeping baby. Looking angry. Prudence hurried into the room and scooped Bonnie up into her arms.

"Time for her midnight feed," she whispered to Zoe, who barely moved from the spot.

Zoe watched her with an unreadable expression.

"Do you want to give her her bottle?" Prudence asked gently.

Zoe declined with a rapid shake of her head.

"Okay, why don't you get some sleep then?"

Prudence carried Bonnie towards the stairs, and Zoe followed close behind. She thought perhaps Zoe had changed her mind, but she remained at the top of the stairs, watching her as she carried the child down. When she reached the bottom, she turned and looked up. Zoe was still standing there. Her arms hung limp by her sides, her young face expressionless. Prudence stared back, but Zoe seemed unable to break her gaze. If she didn't know better, she'd have said Zoe hated her.

Finally, Zoe turned and retreated. Prudence hoped she was going back to sleep. She went into the kitchen and began preparing Bonnie's bottle. It was damned awkward doing so whilst holding Bonnie in her arms, so she set her down on the play mat. Bonnie started to stir, her face scrunched up as she realised she was no longer being held.

"It's okay," Prudence soothed. "Everything's going to be okay."

She waited impatiently for the bottle to warm up, then gave it a quick shake. She picked Bonnie up and held her close as she fed her, wondering what to do about Zoe. There was definitely something wrong with her. She would have to discuss it with Nathan. She just hoped he wouldn't think she was criticising Zoe's parenting skills. If there was one thing she had learned being a nurse all those years, it was that no one was immune to mental illness. Even the most capable people could suffer in silence, and, sadly, too many did.

Once she had fed and changed Bonnie, she carried her back upstairs. Zoe was no longer in the nursery, but the door to her room gave a little creak. It was impossible to tell in the darkness, but Prudence had the feeling that Zoe was standing right behind the door, watching her. Watching Bonnie.

She went into the nursery and lay Bonnie back down in the crib. Normally, she would go straight to bed now, but there was a tight knot in her chest.

"Don't worry," she whispered to the sleeping baby. "I'll keep you company, just in case."

She curled up in the rocking chair. It wasn't the most comfortable way to sleep, but Prudence didn't have much alternative. There was no way she was leaving Bonnie alone tonight.

21

PRUDENCE

The door to Zoe and Nathan's room was closed when Prudence awoke. Bonnie was fast asleep, her little tuft of hair sticking up like a mohawk. Prudence rose to her feet and stood over the cot to check on her. Her cheeks were pink, her breathing regular.

"Right," she murmured. "You stay there, I'll go and get us some drinks."

She padded down to the kitchen and found the kettle warm. The kitchen smelled like toast. Was Zoe up then? She made the drinks quickly and returned to the nursery, setting her tea down on the windowsill and reaching into the cot for Bonnie.

Bonnie guzzled her milk, gazing into Prudence's eyes with adoration. Prudence gazed back. Sometimes, when she was really tired, she could believe it was Nathan she was holding. He'd been such a lovely baby. It had been the best part of her life. She was so grateful to have the chance again, with Bonnie.

"And the best part is that I get to hand you back to your mum and dad when I've had enough," she told Bonnie.

Except that wasn't quite true. Nathan was always at work and Zoe was practically living in her room. Earlier, Prudence had gently suggested a walk and Zoe had looked at her like she'd suggested she take up windsurfing.

Zoe was still in her room when Alana returned the next day, wanting to take Zoe and Bonnie back with her.

"I'm really concerned about Zoe," Prudence told her. "I've arranged for a doctor friend to come out to see her later this afternoon, so I think it's best she stays here for now."

"What Zoe needs is a nice rest at home," Alana argued. "And a few home comforts."

A wrinkle formed on her brow and Prudence wondered if she'd hurt her feelings by turning down her suggestion. Of course, Alana must be as worried as she was.

Prudence bit her lip. "I really think it's more than that. It's very important we get help for Zoe now. It might help for her to talk to someone who isn't family."

"I know my daughter!" Alana objected.

"I know you do," Prudence said gently. "But you need to trust me on this. She isn't herself right now. I know she must be tired, but she's barely even looked at Bonnie these last few days. I really think she needs to see a doctor and then we can take it from there. I'll ring you later to let you know how it goes."

Alana was silent for a moment. Prudence could understand her disappointment, but they had to think about what was best for Zoe. And Bonnie.

Finally, Alana nodded her head. "I'll be off then. Call me straight after and let me know what the doctor says."

Prudence nodded. "I will."

. . .

Frieda was an old colleague from the hospital. They weren't especially close, but she owed Prudence a favour and Prudence respected her opinion.

She sat with Zoe for a while, gently asking her questions, while Prudence left them alone to talk. She didn't expect Frieda to get anywhere with her sitting there, intruding. It could be hard for patients to talk to doctors. Zoe needed space to unload.

When the door opened, Zoe looked a little happier. Prudence couldn't tell if her change in mood was genuine or just an act. Frieda told her that she'd prescribed some antidepressants for Zoe, which Prudence offered to pick up for her.

She thanked Frieda for her time and took Bonnie out with her to get the pills, as she still wasn't confident about leaving Zoe alone with the baby. When she got back, Zoe was sitting in exactly the same place she had left her.

Prudence called Alana as she had promised, and Alana repeated her offer to have Zoe and Bonnie for a few days, but when she asked Zoe, she seemed reluctant.

"I don't want to. I don't want to go anywhere."

She looked so sad, Prudence wanted to hug her.

"Take the pills," she urged. "They'll help you to feel like yourself again."

Zoe took one and swallowed it down with some water.

"That's it," Prudence said. "You'll soon start to feel better."

In reality, she knew it wasn't as simple as that. She just hoped Zoe would be one of the ones the pills would work for.

As the days passed, Zoe seemed a little better. Prudence found her outside in the garden one morning, enjoying the sun. The next day, she even got up and cooked breakfast for everyone before Nathan had to get off to uni.

"She seems a little happier," Prudence commented to Nathan.

"Yes, she is," Nathan said.

He seemed to just assume the pills would work. Everybody did. A part of Prudence remained sceptical about Zoe's progress, but there was another change she'd noticed. Zoe had finally stopped her constant texting. Without the distraction of her phone, she seemed more tuned in to the world around her. She paid more attention to Bonnie and started to react differently when Bonnie cried. Whereas before, she had seemed to find the sound of Bonnie's crying unbearable, now she genuinely wanted to comfort her.

Still Prudence was concerned when she found her dressing Bonnie in her coat one afternoon.

"Where are you going?" she asked.

"Don't look so alarmed. I'm just taking her for a walk."

"Oh, that sounds nice." She glanced out the window. "Do you mind if I tag along?"

They had a pleasant walk along the canal and into the park. It was a sunny day and there were lots of families out walking. Zoe pushed the pram and Prudence walked beside her, noting how natural Zoe looked. She was getting a little colour back in her cheeks. For too long she had resembled a ghost.

Bonnie slept for much of the walk. She was happy as long as they kept moving, but as they completed their circuit of the lake she gave a little startled cry.

"She's probably hungry." There was a slight inflection at the end of Zoe's sentence and her gazed flickered briefly to Prudence, who nodded.

"Yes, I think you're right. We should probably head home."

"Oh, look, isn't that your friend?" Zoe asked, pointing out Heidi at the pavement café.

"So it is!" Prudence waved, and Heidi returned her greeting with enthusiasm.

They walked over to her and she admired Bonnie, who was getting decidedly grumpy now.

Prudence pulled out the change bag. "I've got some ready-made formula in here. I'll just grab the waitress and get her to warm it up."

"Thank you," Zoe said, pulling Bonnie from the pram and settling in an empty chair beside Heidi.

"I'll grab us a couple of lattes while I'm there, shall I?"

"That would be nice," Zoe said. Even her voice seemed better. Softer, lighter.

Zoe bounced Bonnie on her knee and by the time Prudence returned with the formula Bonnie was ready to chug it. Zoe gave Bonnie her bottle, looking every bit the capable mother.

"Where were you yesterday?" Heidi asked, as the waitress brought the lattes.

"At home," Prudence said. "Why?"

"I rang you a couple of times. You didn't answer."

"Oh, maybe I was in the garden."

Zoe was rubbing Bonnie's back now. She looked less awkward when she held her. She was more natural and relaxed. She was finally getting the hang of it, Prudence thought. She ought to be pleased, but she was suspicious of Zoe's sudden turnaround. Was she really feeling better, or was she responding to Prudence's concern? She didn't want Zoe to feel that she had to pretend.

Prudence finished her latte and got to her feet. "If you'll both excuse me for a minute, I need to use the loo."

On her way back from the toilets, Prudence ran into a woman she knew from Zumba. The woman had got wind that Prudence had once been a nurse and she listed a whole host of symptoms for Prudence to speculate about. She even insisted on showing her her chilblains. From where she was standing, Heidi and Zoe seemed to be getting along like a house on fire. Heidi was nodding vigorously. Prudence wondered what they were talking about. She finally extricated herself from her conversation, but by the time she returned to the table Zoe was packing up her things, ready to leave.

22

ZOE

From: Zoe Nithercott <Zoe.Nithercott@lbro.ac.uk>
To: Ted Nithercott <Edward.Nithercott@gmail.com>
Subject: Sorry (again)

Dad,

I didn't mean to make you worry and if I have, I'm sorry. That
was never my intention. Like I said, Bonnie really is a good
baby. She's much more alert now. She follows me around the
room with her eyes and it's like she's trying to talk to me.
She's making shapes with her mouth and one day those
shapes will become words and I'll finally be able to hear her.
I want my little girl to be able to say anything that comes into
her head. I want her to be able to make decisions for herself. I
want her to have a freedom that others have never had. I
never want her to live in ignorance or fear. It's not her fault
the world is so messed up. I just wanted life to be better for

her, for us. Sorry, Dad. I know I'm not explaining myself very well.

I want you to know that everything is under control. It all seemed pretty bleak for a while but I think it's going to be fine. Honestly, I never thought there could be a good outcome to all this but I'm feeling stronger than I've ever felt in my whole life and it's all thanks to Nathan. I'd really like you to meet him, Dad. I really think you'd like him.

Your worry wart,

Zoe xxx

23

PRUDENCE

Prudence set Bonnie down on the playmat and headed for the kitchen to make some toasted sandwiches. She began slicing cheese and tomatoes, then she put it all in the toastie machine to cook. She hoped Zoe would have a sandwich too. Now that she was feeling a little better, her appetite was probably returning.

While she was waiting for the food, she drifted into the lounge and noticed that the phone was off the hook. She lifted the receiver and listened. That was odd. The line was dead. She glanced down and saw that it had come right out of the plug. No wonder she hadn't heard any of Heidi's calls. Never mind, she'd soon fix that.

She and Zoe sat together in the lounge.

"Do you mind if I put on *Strictly*?" she asked.

"Go ahead," said Zoe, glancing down at Bonnie, who was still perfectly content. She was pulling a variety of faces, as if practising different expressions. Zoe burst out laughing.

"She looks so funny!"

Prudence smiled. She really did.

She put on the recording of *Strictly* and Zoe got quite into it. She was very good at picking the winners and had some amusing comments about the costumes. "Is that dress supposed to look like that or has she put it on backwards?"

Prudence snorted. It did indeed look that way.

"Well, what about that other one? What's she wearing? A cauliflower?"

They both giggled and then clapped as the dancers pulled off a particularly tricky manoeuvre.

The rest of the day passed comfortably. It rained for a while, but instead of skulking off to her room Zoe sat with Prudence, watching more TV programmes and enjoying multiple cups of tea.

This is how it should have been from the beginning, Prudence thought with regret. She didn't know why she had got off to such a bad start with Zoe, but Bonnie had finally brought them together and she was glad.

They gave Bonnie her bath after dinner, and Zoe read to her, while Prudence sang her a song she used to sing to Nathan. They each kissed the baby on the cheek and crept out of the room. Prudence was amazed as always when Bonnie went straight to sleep. She was as regular as clockwork, she thought to herself, heading downstairs to do the dishes.

Zoe excused herself, saying she wanted to catch up on some coursework.

"Don't overdo it," Prudence warned. "No one expects you to be all caught up yet."

Zoe nodded and smiled. "I'll probably fall asleep as soon as I open my books," she admitted.

"It's alright if you do."

"Wake me up for Bonnie's next feed," Zoe said.

Prudence nodded, but she would do no such thing. Zoe needed her rest.

She sat down on the sofa and waited for Nathan to get

home. She'd discovered that this was the best time of day to connect with her son. He often came in tired from work, but she'd heat up his dinner and he would eat and they'd talk, then if he wasn't too knackered he'd give Bonnie her midnight feed. He loved doing that. Some days it was the only chance he got to see her. It was a shame, Prudence thought. He and Zoe were far too serious at times. They both needed to learn to ease up a bit and enjoy what they had.

Her programme came to an end and another started. She hoped Nathan would be home soon or she'd have to give Bonnie her midnight feed herself. She went into the kitchen and checked her mobile, but he hadn't texted to say he'd be late. He must be on his way.

Midnight came and went. Prudence fed Bonnie then slept on the sofa, one ear open for Nathan. He might be a grown man now, but she was his mother and she was entitled to worry.

She woke up with a jolt at three in the morning. She checked for Nathan's shoes, his backpack, but there was no sign of him. She went up to his room. Zoe had left the door ajar. He wasn't there.

She returned to the kitchen and rang him but he didn't answer. She left a message: *Nathan, where the hell are you? It's so late.*

Half an hour later she left another one. *Nathan, this isn't funny. If you've broken down somewhere, just leave the car and call yourself a taxi. I'll pay for it when you get home.*

Cold dread swept over her and she considered calling the police. By five she was pacing the house. She couldn't take it anymore. She went upstairs and shook Zoe awake.

"Zoe! Zoe, wake up."

Zoe woke up with a start. "Bonnie?"

"No, it's Nathan. He hasn't come home. Did he say

anything to you about where he was going? Could he have stayed with one of his friends?"

"I don't know anything. He hasn't called." Zoe was out of bed in a flash. She strode across the room to the dresser where her phone was charging.

"I haven't got any missed calls," she said. "Maybe his phone got stolen?"

Prudence bit down on her knuckles. "Call his friends, work colleagues, his boss. Anyone you can think of."

Zoe set to work. Prudence waited while she spoke with someone.

"That was Bradley. He hasn't seen him, but he'll ring his manager and see if he knows anything."

She dialled another number, but this time whoever it was didn't pick up. She left a message and went straight to the next one. Finally, she'd run out of numbers.

"No one's seen him. He left work at half past eleven. He should have been home the normal time. Do you think he's broken down?"

"But if he's broken down, then why doesn't he call?"

"Maybe his phone's out of charge?"

"Maybe it's been stolen," Prudence said grimly. "What time is it now?"

Zoe checked her phone. "Quarter past seven."

"Right. People should be waking up. Someone has to know where he's got to."

Prudence felt like her head was going to explode. "Are you sure he hasn't rung you? Texted? Anything."

"No. I told you he hasn't."

Zoe sat for a moment, held her head in her hands, then jolted upwards.

"What?"

"We can track his phone."

"How?"

"He has the 'find my phone' app." She tapped at her phone and waited a moment.

Prudence leaned over her shoulder. "Where is he?"

Zoe furrowed her brow. "He's ... he's here. I mean, his phone is. It's in this street."

"Where?"

Zoe pointed. From the location, it looked like Nathan was next door at Jon's house.

"What would he be doing there?"

"I don't know. Maybe he dropped his phone and Jon found it."

"Then where's Nathan?"

Prudence couldn't take it anymore. She pulled on her shoes and marched out of the house. Zoe started to follow, but she waved her back. "Someone has to stay with Bonnie."

Prudence marched up Jon's garden path and pounded on his door. He answered without his trademark glasses. He was wrapped in an old flannel dressing gown and his hair looked damp.

"Have you seen Nathan?" Prudence demanded.

"No, can't say I have."

Prudence bit back her impatience. "He didn't come home last night."

Jon scratched his head. "Well, he's not here then, is he?"

Prudence opened her mouth to say something else, but Jon was already closing the door.

"Do you think he was lying?" Zoe said, when Prudence returned.

"No. I think he was just confused."

Their neighbour on the other side looked out. She was a grey-haired woman, new to the street. Probably very nice, but Prudence hadn't got round to meeting her.

"Excuse me!"

They both looked at her.

"You were asking about your son?"

"Yes."

"I might be mistaken, but I thought I heard his car last night. Would have been in the early hours. I have the misfortune of being a very light sleeper and I was awoken by the beam of light through my curtains."

Prudence looked at Zoe, who stared back at her. All at once, she was filled with an almighty dread. She staggered towards the garage and pulled on the handle. It opened with a loud creak.

"Nathan?"

As she ventured into the garage, a sick sense told her that something was very wrong. The moment she registered the car, she expected to see him sitting in the driver's seat. He must have been tired when he came home. Most likely he'd fallen asleep. But the front seat was empty, the windows rolled down a little to let in the air. She caught the whiff of whisky as she peered into the back seat and that's where she saw him.

"God! Oh god!"

24

PRUDENCE

She barely recognised the bloated figure sprawled out on the back seat. He was a hideous caricature of himself. His tongue had swollen badly and caused his jaw to gape, and his eyes bulged nearly out of their sockets. His entire body was contorted and disfigured.

Her knees wobbled beneath her, and she leaned against the seat to steady herself.

"Nathan!" she moaned softly. She wanted to cradle him in her arms, but she knew she must look for signs of life. A heartbeat, a pulse.

There was none.

She stroked his cheek and found that it was warm to the touch. Her mind flashed to an image of rubbing suntan lotion on his back. He had always burned so easily, but it wasn't the sun that had done the damage this time. His fingers were cold and blue, and his hand sprang back into place the moment she let it go.

Her vision blurred and a great lump of grief wedged itself in her throat. That was the last thing she knew before she fell backwards. She was vaguely aware of someone pulling her away, a voice in her ear warning her of the fumes. Then she was lying on the grass in front of her house.

Zoe was fighting Jon, trying to punch her way into the garage.

"No, Zoe. You don't want to see him. It's not right."

"Get away from him!" Prudence muttered under her breath, but no one seemed to hear her. The entire neighbourhood was out there, waiting, watching. Like this was some kind of extravaganza.

Blue lights swamped her vision. There were vehicles and voices, an army in breathing apparatus and hazmat suits. Someone was shining a light at her. She flung her arm over her eyes.

"You shouldn't be out here, Mrs Ahern. Someone take her into the house!"

FIVE MINUTES LATER, she lay in a foetal position on the sofa and the house crawled with police.

"Please, someone. Tell me what happened."

She got another flash of Nathan and those awful bulging eyes. It had to be a mistake. It couldn't be her Nathan. It couldn't.

"It looks like carbon monoxide poisoning." The policeman had removed his hat, she noticed. Was that what they did when somebody died?

No! It couldn't be true, could it?

"The garage doors were shut and he'd left the engine on."

"The engine wasn't on!" she protested.

The policeman looked at his colleague. "Well, the battery would be flat now."

"No, he couldn't have!"

"I'm afraid it's true. Is there anyone we can call for you?"

She thought of Frank.

"She has a friend called Heidi," Zoe said. "Her number will be on her phone."

Prudence glanced over at her. Zoe sounded clear and calm, but her lips quivered.

Time shifted in a series of words and shadows. Then Heidi was there, and she was crying, mascara streaked down her face. Zoe was crying too, wailing in Heidi's arms, while Prudence sat stiffly beside them. She couldn't take it anymore and stumbled up the stairs towards her bedroom. She froze as soon as she saw Nathan's room.

She stole him. She stole my son.

Somehow, she forced her body to keep moving, feeling along the wall with her hands until she reached her own room. She rattled the door handle and pulled it open like a drunk. She slammed it furiously behind her and staggered over to the bed. She didn't care if the police had more questions. She needed oblivion.

She went through her medical bag and pulled out a box of sleeping pills she had acquired on the job. She was tempted to take them all, but she only had a small stash and it was going to have to last, so she swallowed one and lay down on the bed.

The pill did the trick. She slept for a long time, then jerked awake, convinced it had all been a terrible dream. Memories came flooding back and the realisation hit her all over again. She saw her son's swollen, distorted face and collapsed back against the pillows, choked with fresh sobs.

The police presence had dwindled by the time she ventured back downstairs. There was one lone policewoman who sat in the corner and another who was making tea in the kitchen. Bonnie slept in her Moses basket next to Heidi.

Prudence spotted Zoe out in the garden, watching her through the glass doors.

"How are you feeling?" Heidi asked softly.

Prudence let out a bitter laugh. "How do you think? I can't get the image out of my mind. The smell too. It was like vinegar or fermented beer or something."

Heidi drew a breath. "It sounds to me like he'd been drinking. Perhaps he fell asleep in the garage when he got home. He was a new father, and you've said yourself he was working very hard, he must have been so tired."

Her soft, familiar face was filled with compassion.

"No," Prudence shook her head adamantly. "He wasn't daft. He knew better than to leave the exhaust running. Someone did this to him. Someone who wanted him out of the way."

Heidi reached for her and held her close. "I don't know what happened," she said softly. "I just want to make it better. You don't deserve this and nor does Zoe. You need to help each other now, to be all you can for Bonnie. Don't you see that? She's all that matters now."

Prudence rose from the sofa and let herself into the kitchen, where a policeman was writing something in his notebook. He'd introduced himself earlier, she remembered.

"You're PC Grainger, aren't you?"

"I am."

"I need to talk to you. It's Zoe. I think she killed my son."

He looked troubled. "Now, that's a very serious allegation."

"I know it sounds far-fetched but hear me out. She must have locked him in the car, or in the garage and turned on the ignition. I don't know the exact mechanics of it. Things have been difficult ever since she came along. The last couple of days were different. I thought we were sailing out of the fog, but she was just setting me up for this, the biggest fall of all.

She pretends to be upset, to cry like she did when Bob died. But she did it. I'm telling you, it was her."

Grainger looked up from his notebook. "Who's Bob?"

"Bob was my dog. She let him out of the garden. He was knocked down in the road."

"When was this?"

"About four months ago now. I mean it, you need to speak to her. I'm sure she's behind all this. In fact, I'm certain of it."

PC Grainger went back into the lounge and talked to Zoe. He sounded calm and sympathetic. He wasn't going to arrest her, Prudence realised. He believed her. They all did. Even Heidi.

The police left the house, not all at once, but in a parade of comings and goings. At some point, Prudence realised they were alone. She leaned back against the sofa, nursing a cup of tea Heidi had made her. Zoe sat slumped on the sofa opposite, rocking the sleeping Bonnie, making out she actually knew what she was doing. That's when the phone rang.

Heidi was the one to answer it. "It's for you, Zoe. It's your mum."

Zoe stood up and handed Bonnie over to Heidi. She held the phone to her ear, but her mum did most of the talking. Prudence watched her like a hawk. Apparently, Alana already knew about Nathan.

"What are you going to do about her?" Heidi asked, in a low voice.

"I don't want her here," Prudence said unhappily. "I can't stand the sight of her."

"But if you kick her out, you'll lose Bonnie too."

"I know." Prudence held her head in her hands. She couldn't lose Bonnie. Her granddaughter was all she had left.

Heidi leaned back against the cushions. "For what it's worth, I think you're wrong about Zoe. I saw her and Nathan together and she wasn't faking it. She loved him, Pru. I don't know what happened to Nathan, but I don't think Zoe had anything to do with it and the sooner you accept that, the better for both of you."

THE FOLLOWING MORNING, Zoe stood at the kitchen counter, slicing bread from an uncut loaf. The knife glistened as she pointed it downwards. She was slicing way too close to her thumb. Prudence approached carefully, unsure what to say. They hadn't been properly alone since Nathan died.

Zoe eyed her warily. "So what now? Are you going to chuck me out?"

Prudence swallowed hard. "You and Bonnie are welcome to stay. After all, this is your home."

Zoe swivelled her head. "I know you don't care about me. You only care about Bonnie. I know about the paternity test, Prudence. I bet you thought you were really clever, hiding it in the outside bin like that."

"I'm not going to defend my actions," Prudence said. "Once she was born, it was obvious that Bonnie was indeed Nathan's, which is just what he always insisted. But if there had been even a shadow of doubt, I wouldn't have thought twice about using it. I did what I did to protect my son."

"Fat lot of good that did him."

Zoe raised the knife just a fraction of an inch and Prudence felt an intense rush of fear. One slash of that knife and she could be dead. But it wasn't her own death that frightened her. She thought of Bonnie, all alone on her play-mat. What would become of her if Zoe killed her? Would Zoe kill Bonnie too? Zoe's bottom lip wobbled as she set down the knife. She looked at the bread she had sliced but did not pick it up and eat it. Perhaps, like Prudence, she was too nauseated to eat. It was hard to tell. Her son's girlfriend was impossible to read. Was she devastated by the loss of Nathan, or was she feeling defensive about what she had done? Worse still, did she even remember?

"WAS THAT THE DOORBELL?" Zoe asked.

Prudence nodded. "I'll get it."

Caroline and Jackie stood awkwardly on the doorstep. Prudence should have invited them in but she didn't want to. She couldn't deal with the rituals of making the tea and listening to platitudes. She knew her friends meant well, but they would never be able to understand her grief. Nothing like this had ever happened to them.

"We won't stay long," Caroline said, sensing her mood. "We just wanted to let you know that we're here, if ever you need us."

Jackie nodded. This was the longest she'd ever been silent. It would be funny, if it weren't so painful. "Let me know if you need any shopping or anything," she said.

"I just want my son back," Prudence burst out. She hadn't meant to say anything. The last thing she wanted was a conversation, but the words just spilled from her mouth. "I feel like I let him down."

"You didn't let him down," Jackie said.

"I'm his mother. It was my job to protect him, to keep him safe."

Caroline took her hand and squeezed it.

"You did everything you could for him, but even you couldn't protect him from his thoughts."

Prudence was aghast. "Is that what you think? That he killed himself?"

They looked at each other, uncertain.

"But Heidi said ..."

"Heidi doesn't know anything. The coroner will make a report. Then we'll all know the truth."

Prudence stopped answering the door after that. She crawled into bed with her laptop. She wanted to find the one person who was supposed to be there, sharing her grief. Frank had been as good as his word. He'd sent her paternity cheques every month for the first two years of Nathan's life. She hadn't cashed a single one of them because she was trying to prove to him that it wasn't his money she was after. She had prayed that he would come back. She'd been full of hope back then. Perhaps he would make a surprise appearance on Nathan's birthday, or he'd pop in for Christmas with a present, but he did none of those things and eventually the cheques stopped coming, too. She didn't even have a phone number for him anymore. Somewhere along the line he'd changed it and hadn't let her know. She'd kept an eye on him, of course. She knew from his Twitter account that he was working at a medical laboratory in Edinburgh. So much for his dream of becoming a surgeon.

She logged on and checked his account. There were no updates. He had seventy-three followers. He didn't tweet much but when he did, the same person always responded. Prudence clicked on her profile and felt a fresh tide of loss:

Maura Grant, mother of two. She'd posted a picture of herself and her two children mucking about in their garden, and standing beside them, smiling broadly, was Frank. She looked more closely at the picture. They had the same eyes as Nathan. She let out a great puff of air.

She had misunderstood, all this time. It wasn't that Frank didn't want children. He just didn't want them with her. Furiously, she scanned Maura's information but there was no email address and no phone number. She so badly wanted to contact him, not to tell him about Nathan and Bonnie but to punish him for not wanting her.

For hours, she trawled websites, looking for stories of people who had died like her son. She read everything she could get her hands on but still couldn't find any answers and every time she closed her eyes, all she saw was Nathan, his wild eyes begging her for help.

DESPITE HER OBJECTIONS, Nathan's death was ruled a suicide. There was an article about it in the paper. Prudence stumbled upon it quite by accident, and that was her day gone, staring at his beautiful face. Where had they even got this picture? Had Zoe given it to them? Prudence certainly hadn't.

She found more articles online and read each one compulsively, poring over the words for clues. Journalists were supposed to be good at sniffing out a story. But these ones just repeated one another, almost word for word. It was like nobody thought for themselves anymore. One of the articles had a comments section. People had written in, saying how sad Nathan's death was. People who knew him said what a nice person he was. People she hadn't thought of for ages, like a teacher from primary school and a friend from when he'd been in the Scouts. One person had written that suicide was a coward's way out.

She should have known better, but she replied:

My son did not kill himself.

The reply came back instantly:

Yes he did and you should too.

She stared at it in horror, but a moment later it was gone. Most likely a moderator had seen it and taken it down. She tilted back her chair. Her eyes were hot and sunken, and even the effort of blinking felt like a chore.

She glanced at her watch. It was time to feed Bonnie

again. Zoe had relinquished all responsibility for her again, not that Prudence really minded. Looking after Bonnie was about the only thing keeping her going.

Over the next few days, she picked up the phone and spoke with Nathan's friends, co-workers and lecturers, who all thought he had been happy if tired. No one thought he wasn't coping. They had all thought he seemed really invested in his future.

Zoe spent her days moping about the house. She made a really good impression of a heartbroken widow and Prudence didn't know what to think. She veered between feeling sorry for Zoe and almost wanting to strangle her. If she wasn't responsible for Nathan's death, she still knew more than she let on, but she refused to talk.

Heidi came over to help her with the funeral arrangements. It was all so painful.

"You never expect to bury your son," Prudence said, flicking through the casket brochure with distaste. She didn't want to make these decisions. She didn't want to bury him at all.

"What does Zoe think?" Heidi asked.

"Like she cares," Prudence said. "She'd go for the cheapest one. She's a born Scrooge, that girl."

"Well, what about the flowers? Surely she has an opinion about those?"

Heidi called Zoe downstairs and had her look at the samples. Zoe looked over each of them but couldn't make up her mind.

"What do you think?" she asked Heidi.

"I want to know what you think," Heidi said, with a slight smile.

"I don't know," Zoe said sadly.

"Something not right there," Heidi said, once Zoe had returned to her room.

"Tell me about it," said Prudence.

As Heidi was leaving, Jon popped his head in from next door. Prudence couldn't recall speaking to him since the day Nathan had died, but then he wasn't much of a conversationalist.

"So I was thinking about what I could do for you," he said, getting straight to the point.

"Oh?"

"Well, it strikes me that your garden's getting a bit overgrown now, so I thought I'd volunteer to give it a tidy-up."

"That's very kind of you but—" She paused. *Why not let him help?* It wasn't as if she had the energy.

"Only, my mower's still broken. I was going to get Nathan to have a look at it but—"

Jon's eyes flickered. "Say no more."

He walked out to the shed and opened the door. She had a padlock but never bothered to actually lock it. There was nothing much in there besides the mower and a heap of garden junk.

Jon returned ten minutes later, looking even more serious than usual. "Well, now you know what the problem is, don't you?"

"Do I?"

"It's been wired wrong. That's why it gave you a shock. I'd say you were lucky the damage wasn't worse."

Prudence frowned. "But I've been using that mower for years. It was always fine. I mean, there was a bit of a problem a while ago, but Nathan fixed that. He was an engineering student. He knew what he was doing."

Jon shook his head. "Then I can't understand how he could have made such a mistake because I'm telling you, that mower is wired wrong. It's easy enough to fix but as it stands right now that thing's a death trap."

25

PRUDENCE

Prudence remained out in the garden, the facts rattling around in her head. What should she do?

She'd long had the sense that Zoe wanted to get rid of her. She'd definitely been messing with her, like the time she'd stolen her towel, but what if her real intended target had been Nathan all along? He was the one who had done most of the lawnmowing. She'd only stepped in because he'd been so busy. Zoe couldn't have known Prudence would be the one to get electrocuted, and when that didn't work, she'd tried something else. Zoe must have waited up for Nathan that fateful night. She must have slipped outside to meet him. He had been drinking, the toxicology report said, but the Nathan she knew would never drink and drive. Had he and Zoe been drinking together in the garage after he came home? Had she seen to it that he was so drunk that he couldn't get out of the car? But why had the engine been left on? Wouldn't he have noticed? Or had she done that only after he fell asleep on the back seat?

With her usual impeccable timing, Heidi appeared at the gate.

"Hello! Zoe said I'd find you out here."

Prudence looked around to check Zoe hadn't followed her out, then she told Heidi what Jon had discovered.

"Don't you see? This is proof," Prudence said grimly. "Proof that Nathan's death wasn't an accident. Proof that Zoe was trying to kill him."

"But where's her motive?" Heidi objected. "I agree it looks odd that Nathan would make such a lethal mistake, but he was working very hard. Don't you think it's more likely he simply screwed up?"

"No!" Prudence banged her fist down on the bench. "I can't believe that. It had to be Zoe."

"I just think you're wrong about her. If someone did sabotage your lawnmower, then I don't think it was Zoe. I'm still convinced she loved Nathan and he loved her."

Prudence let her shoulders droop. She had been so fired up, but now she wasn't sure. "Do you think I should report it to the police?"

"You've still got the funeral to get through."

"Don't remind me." Whenever she thought about the funeral, she felt a new wave of panic. "I'm not sure if I'm going to go."

"Are you serious?"

"I don't know if I can face all those people. And the thought of seeing his coffin. My little boy trapped in a wooden box. It makes me feel sick."

"You don't have to go if you don't want to, but for what it's worth, I think you should."

"So what do I do?"

"I think it can wait another day," Heidi said. "Give yourself a chance to grieve. You need to make sure you're right about Zoe, because if you're wrong you would be making things a whole lot worse."

· · ·

THE DAY of the funeral loomed wet and windy, as if the gods were angry and wanted revenge, but by the time they reached the church, the sun was peeking through the clouds. Zoe sat silently in the back of Heidi's car, Bonnie in her car seat beside her. Prudence wondered if it would be too macabre to take pictures. She had so few of Nathan with Bonnie. Perhaps they should take one of her with the coffin so that Bonnie would know she had been there.

They got out of the car, and Prudence took a few faltering steps forward, then stopped. Beside her, Zoe looked equally uncertain. Nobody liked a funeral. It meant confronting death head on, looking into the eyes of the beast and waiting to see who would blink first.

"I don't want to go in," Zoe said.

Prudence closed her eyes and opened them again. "We have to. For Nathan."

The back of the church was taken up by teenagers dressed not in band T-shirts but proper suits, and many of them even wore ties. She recognised Nathan's best friend, Bradley, sitting in a separate row with his mother, who was weeping softly. Prudence understood that she was not crying for Nathan, who she had barely known, but at the way this tragedy had affected her own life – the very thought that this could have been her son.

Heidi went to talk to the vicar while Prudence and Zoe sat in the front row. They wedged the baby carrier between them like the Berlin Wall. Prudence tried to focus her attention on Bonnie, but it was impossible to ignore the fact that Zoe's shoulders were shaking. Was it the guilt that was getting to her, or was she overcome with grief?

The vicar spoke warmly about Nathan, but his words were like lasers through her heart. His life was just beginning. There was no way of putting a positive spin on that. He had worked so hard, but he would never graduate. He had met the love of his life, but they would never marry. He had become a father, but he would never see his child grow up. There was no poetry, no justice, only sorrow.

Heidi did a reading from the Bible and then Prudence said a few words, thanking everyone for coming. She invited them all to come to the wake at the Fox and Hound afterwards. As she sat back down, Zoe rose from her seat.

"May I say a few words?"

No, Prudence wanted to yell, but Heidi lay a warning hand on her arm.

"Let her."

Zoe got up and went to the front. She looked gaunt and nervous. Her hair was pulled back in a tight ponytail that made her face look too thin. She gazed around the room with a sad smile.

"I guess you're all here because you loved Nathan," she stated. "I didn't know him for as long as some of you" – her eyes flicked to Prudence – "but I can promise you, I loved him with all my heart ..."

She talked about the first time she'd met Nathan. How she had walked into the wrong lecture theatre and sat down beside him. A few minutes into the lecture, she had realised her mistake but by then the professor was looking at her. Perhaps he knew she hadn't attended any of his other lectures and thought she was lazy. For whatever reason, he put her on the spot.

"He asked me the most impossible questions," Zoe said, eyes sparkling with laughter. "Fortunately, I had sat next to Nathan. He whispered the answers in my ear. To thank him, I offered to buy him a beer afterwards. I thought we'd go to the pub on campus, but Nathan said he knew a better place. He took me to the acoustic club in town. I loved it. It was open mic night and the music was really good. Right at the end, Nathan borrowed a guitar. He played *With or Without You* by

U2, one of my favourite songs of all time. I thought he was really talented, but he admitted afterwards that he could only play three songs. I asked him what the other songs were and he told me they were *Baa Baa Black Sheep* and *Three Blind Mice*. I made him get back up there and play me *Three Blind Mice*, and he did and he added this ridiculous guitar solo and it was terrible."

Tears were streaming down her face now, tears of laughter, tears of pain. Zoe glanced over at Bonnie and grew sombre. "I can't believe there won't be any more nights like that," she said sadly. "I can't believe he won't be here for Bonnie's first day at school or to walk her down the aisle. But my greatest fear is that I'm going to forget him. I have less than a year's worth of memories, and there's no way to download them. Every day, the colours and sounds become more muted, and I start to ask myself, did it really happen that way or was it different? And I can't check with Nathan, because he's gone."

Prudence exhaled and Heidi passed her a tissue. The door opened loudly and Alana crept in. Prudence turned to watch as she walked down the aisle, looking for an empty seat. Zoe did not look at her mother. She continued with her speech, which grew even more emotional. Prudence couldn't work out if she was a brilliant actor or if she was genuine. She glanced back at Alana again. She sat with her head bowed as if in prayer, or so Prudence thought until she saw the phone in her lap. Was she ... texting? Alana must have sensed Prudence watching because her head shot up. Their eyes locked and in that instant, everything changed.

Prudence saw that Alana was completely unmoved. In fact, she looked positively bored, glancing down to examine her fingernails, stifling a yawn. She was wearing black but her outfit was designer, the top low cut. She seemed incapable of toning it down. Prudence's lips tightened. A vein pulsed on the side of her face.

Alana noticed her looking and immediately altered her expression. She dabbed at her eyes and let the hair fall over her face, but it was too late. Prudence had seen the slip. When Zoe finished her speech, she came and sat in her original place next to Prudence and Bonnie. Alana shuffled down several seats so that she was now sitting in the pew behind.

The vicar was concluding the service: "Nathan, we bless your memory with the greatest love for you. Go your way in peace and may your memory be a blessing to all who ..."

"Psst! Zoe!" Alana's voice was loud enough to attract attention. Zoe darted a worried glance her way.

"Time to go," Alana said, tapping her watch.

Zoe's eyes grew wild and she glanced back at the vicar, but he seemed to have finished speaking.

"Didn't you hear me? Show's over. Let's hit the road."

"Wait a minute, where are you going?" Prudence asked Zoe.

Zoe looked at Alana. She seemed paralysed, unable to speak for herself. With a sick feeling in her stomach, Prudence realised that Alana had allowed Zoe to attend the funeral to say goodbye and now she expected to leave with her. Not just Zoe, but Bonnie too.

Alana caught Prudence staring and her face broke into a fake grin. "Didn't Zoe tell you? I'm taking my girls home with me."

Prudence looked at Zoe. "Is that what you want, Zoe? You know you and Bonnie are very welcome to stay on at my place."

She couldn't keep the begging tone out of her voice. Zoe couldn't even meet her eyes. She stood gingerly and lifted Bonnie's carrier. The baby gave a little wail of protest, then mother and daughter walked out of the church.

As the door closed behind them, Prudence cried in earnest. She'd thought losing Nathan was as bad as it could possibly get, but this new ache in her heart was all for Bonnie.

Heidi took her arm and steered her out of the church.

Prudence felt a great pressure in her chest, as if a wave had hit the sea wall. She tried to focus, darting a desperate glance around the car park, but there was no sign of Alana's flashy blue car. Or her pink one, for that matter.

The congregation were following them out of the church. There were so many people there, all wanting to pay their respects.

"I can't do it," she told Heidi. "I ... I have to go."

"Prudence!"

Heidi tried to take her arm, but Prudence pushed her old friend away.

"Prudence!"

It wasn't Heidi this time, but Nathan's friend, Bradley. She pretended not to hear him as she scurried out of the gate and back to the house, where she could finally grieve alone.

Brring! Brring!

    Sleepily, Prudence grabbed the phone.

    "Hello?"

"Hi, Mum."

She bolted upright. "Who is this?"

"It's me."

"Nathan? It ... it can't be ..."

Oh, but that voice!

There was a crackle on the other end of the line.

"I've just been for a job interview. In New Zealand."

Prudence rubbed her eyes. "New Zealand? Why so far away?"

"You should see the view here, it's incredible! I can see a fruiting tamarillo tree through my bedroom window."

"Nathan, I found your body. You were ..."

"They've offered me my dream job. The pay's really good, and I don't even have to finish uni. I can start right away."

"I can't believe this! I ... I'll go straight to the airport and get the next flight out. I can be there tomorrow."

"There's a catch. You can't ever visit me."

"Why? Why not? Why not, Nathan?"

"I'm sorry, I have to go now."

The phone beeped.

"Are you using a payphone? Put in another pound."

The beeping grew more insistent. It felt as though the sound was coming from inside her ears.

"Nathan? Nathan!"

Prudence opened her eyes and realised that the phone was actually ringing. It would be Heidi, checking up on her, but she just wasn't in the mood to take it. She shook her head to shake off the remnants of sleep. Her head felt heavy, and her neck and scalp muscles were tight. That was what she got for sleeping on the sofa, she supposed. She must have collapsed there when she got home, too exhausted to make it up the stairs.

She thought back to her dream. It had felt nice to speak to Nathan, even if it was just a dream. Her mother had died a few years ago, but she had never visited Prudence in a dream. That was typical, she supposed. When her mother had been alive, she had always expected Prudence to be the one to visit.

She looked around the room, trying to take comfort in the familiar four walls. She was greeted with utter silence. Even the birds chirped quietly outside the window.

Restless, she trudged upstairs. She paused in front of Nathan and Zoe's room, but she couldn't make herself go in. Instead, she went into the nursery, where Bonnie's stuffed tiger lay on the freshly made bed. A neat pile of clean baby clothes sat on the shelf, waiting to be put away. Zoe hadn't taken any of it.

She picked up Bonnie's tiger and hugged it to her chest, unable to get Alana's nasty face out of her mind. How could she do this? On the day of Nathan's funeral. It was an unnatural act of cruelty. How much pain was a mother supposed to bear?

She went into her own room and rang Zoe, but there was no answer.

She left a voicemail: "Hello Zoe, this is Prudence. I just wanted to check you were okay? You and Bonnie. Please know that I still care about you both and I'm worried. If you need anything, you know where I am. I'll leave you alone now. We all grieve in our own way, but I'd like to come and visit on Sunday. I'll bring some of Bonnie's things. You've left all her clothes here and her cuddly tiger. I'm sure she's missing him, and well ... me."

Zoe did not return her call and it now occurred to her that she didn't know where Alana lived. She tried the phone book but Alana was not listed. There was no mention of her on the electoral register, either. She typed the name Alana Nithercott into a search engine and found a link to a newspaper article all about Alana. She had been named Estate Agent of the Year at her company, apparently.

She noted the address of the branch. It was based in a small village. Alana had to live somewhere in the surrounding area. She thought for a minute, then found a community board for the village on Facebook.

"I've just received a parcel for a Mrs A Nithercott," she typed. "Can anyone tell me the correct address?"

Within minutes, three people had answered to say that Alana Nithercott lived in Russet Way. Number six, a fourth person informed her.

"Thank you," Prudence typed. "I will see to it that it reaches its rightful owner."

She pulled up a map and studied the area carefully, noting how neat the lawns looked. Yes, it looked exactly the kind of place where Alana would live. She pictured Bonnie in her pristine pink nursery. How Nathan had laughed at that. No one was laughing now.

She rang the police about the lawnmower and PC Grainger came and took down a report. He was kind and concerned but didn't respond with the urgency she had hoped for.

She lay low for the rest of the week, compulsively watching reality TV shows and eating the chocolates Heidi posted through her door. Heidi left her proper food too, easy things she could heat up in the microwave, but Prudence couldn't be bothered. She stuffed the meals in the freezer and lived on peanuts and crackers. By the end of the week, her cupboards were depleted but her spirits rose at the prospect of seeing Bonnie.

A local car dealership had dropped off a hire car for her. It was a sensible Toyota, much nicer than her old car, the one Nathan had died in. The police still had that. She'd told them she didn't want it back. She would buy a new one, once she was feeling up to it.

She rang both Zoe and Alana before setting off on Sunday morning but neither answered the phone. Over the course of the long drive, she wondered what kind of house they lived in. Despite Alana's flashy cars, she had a feeling they weren't as well off as they made out. In her experience, rich people rarely thought about money, whereas Zoe was obsessed. She suspected that Alana merely borrowed or hired her fancy cars. Her clothes looked expensive too, but for all Prudence knew, she bought them in the sales.

It had been a long time since she had driven this far. Dark clouds were forming in the sky and she felt the heaviness in her temples, as though there was a tight band wrapped around her head. She tried calling Zoe one more time, but still there was no answer.

Presently, she turned into Russet Way. A cluster of

detached houses had been built around a perfect patch of green. There wasn't a single child to be seen anywhere in the street. She double-checked her address book. Alana lived at number six, the house with the purple door.

She was pleased to hear voices inside. Good. That meant they were home. She rang the bell and waited. She was about to ring it again when she heard the latch being pulled back. Slowly, Zoe eased the door open and peered through the gap. Her hair was limp and her face ashen. Her gaze jumped around like she had difficulty focusing.

"You can't come in."

"Just a few minutes. Please! I've driven all this way."

"You have to go. You're no longer a part of this family."

Prudence opened her mouth to protest but Zoe clutched her hand and gripped it so tight she thought she'd draw blood.

"Trust me, it's better this way." She let her hand fall and turned her head for a moment. She murmured something unintelligible.

"Is your mum there?" Prudence asked. "Can I speak to her?"

"No! You have to go now. You have to leave us alone."

Prudence shook her head. "I'm not going anywhere until I see Bonnie."

"Then I'm afraid we'll have to call the police."

Zoe slammed the door so suddenly Prudence had to jump out of the way. She pounded on it.

"Let me in!"

A plop of rain landed on her shoulder.

A woman looked out of one of the neighbouring houses and shook her head in disproval.

Prudence pounded and pounded, but nothing changed. "I'll be speaking to my lawyer," she threatened.

She took a faltering step towards her car but couldn't

seem to make her legs work so she folded herself onto the doorstep. She held her head in her hands, her vision blurred with rain and tears. When she finally lifted her head, she saw Zoe watching her through the rain-splattered window.

27

PRUDENCE

B radley's car was on the driveway when Prudence arrived home. *He's probably here to see Nathan,* she thought before she caught herself.

She tucked her hair behind her ear, aware that she must look a state. She was exhausted from the long drive and her body felt clammy and disgusting. She forced a smile, all the same.

"Hi, Bradley. How are you?"

"I'm ... I'm fine, Mrs ... Prudence. I just wanted to ..."

Prudence looked at him with sympathy. Bradley had always been a nervous boy, not as confident as the rest of Nathan's friends. But oh, so polite. Growing up, he was the one who would come and help her bake flapjacks while the others were playing computer games or arguing about which superhero was the toughest. He was good at it, too. He knew exactly how much syrup to add, and his little face would light up if she let him lick the spoon.

"Do you want to come inside?" she asked.

Much as she wanted to be alone, she was fond of him and felt bad about running off after the funeral.

"If that's okay with you."

She led him into the house and put the kettle on, making a cup of tea for herself and a hot chocolate for Bradley. He still had a sweet tooth, it seemed.

They sat at the kitchen table and talked about everything except Nathan. Bradley was still single, she tactfully gathered. Still liking uni, although there was way too much coursework.

"There was something," he said at last, pushing the hair out of his eyes. "You asked me if Nathan was himself in the days before he ..."

Prudence tensed, not daring to interrupt.

"I heard something at uni. There's a rumour going round ..."

She fought the urge to shake him. She wished he would get to the point.

"People are saying that he was out in Nottingham the night he died. He was seen in a bar. They're saying he was seeing someone behind Zoe's back."

Prudence shook her head. "Well, that's just not possible. Nathan was besotted with Zoe. He was working every minute he had to provide for her and Bonnie. He was "

Never here?

She inhaled deeply, unsure what to think. She looked at Bradley. His face had turned pink.

"Wouldn't he have said something to you if he was seeing someone else?"

He looked down at his hands. "We used to be really tight, but lately ... I hadn't seen much of him."

Prudence nodded. "Yeah, I'd noticed. Any idea which bar this was?"

Bradley shifted in his seat. "I don't know exactly."

"Can you find out?"

"I'll try."

She questioned him further, but he was unable to provide any more details.

"I need you to find out more," she told him. "It could be very important. I don't believe for a minute that my son killed himself. Whoever it was he met that night, she will have the answers I'm looking for."

Bradley got to his feet and placed his cup in the sink. "I don't want to let you down, Prudence."

She laid a hand on his shoulder. "I believe in you. I've always believed in you."

After he left, she took a shower and closed the blackout blinds in her room. She thought about taking a sleeping pill but she only had one left. She lay down on her bed, but the longed-for sleep never came.

BRADLEY RANG HER LATER. "It was the Light Bar," he said. "Only it's not really a bar, more of a club."

"Thank you," she said, noting this down. She'd never heard of the Light Bar, had no idea what kind of a place it was, but she intended to find out.

"Thank you. I'll go there now."

"You might want to wait a bit. They don't open till nine and, er, there's a dress code. No ripped jeans or trainers."

She allowed herself a small smile. "Thank you. I'll try to remember that."

At a quarter to nine, Prudence drove into a disused industrial estate.

"Stupid satnav," she muttered, typing the address into her mobile phone. But the address was right. This had to be the place. Cautiously, she stepped out of her car. The building in front of her was certainly large enough to be a nightclub but it looked more like a hosiery factory, and judging from the insignia on the wall it probably had been, once.

The car park was virtually empty. Apparently, it wasn't the done thing to arrive early. She rang the bell and a trendy youth came to the door.

"We're not open yet."

"Wait!" Prudence called him back. "It's about my dead son."

He DIDN'T SAY a word to suggest that he'd even heard her, but he wiggled his fingers in a manner that suggested she could follow him inside. A set of sticky stairs led up to a large dance floor with a bar on either side. Staff were hard at work, carrying crates of beer and setting up the tills.

The youth who'd let her in seemed to forget she was there. He drifted into the manager's office and flirted with the woman behind the desk. Prudence waited patiently for a moment, then headed over to one of the bars.

"Excuse me," she said to the bartender.

"Sorry, I'm not allowed to serve yet."

She pulled out her mobile phone. "This is my son, Nathan," she said, showing the man a picture.

"Not my type."

"He died," she told him, with a slight catch in her voice. "This is the last place he was seen alive."

She had his attention now.

"I'm told he came in here with a woman. Or perhaps he met her in here. I don't know." She showed him the picture again. "I don't suppose you recognise him?"

He had a good look. "No. Sorry. We do get a lot of people in here, especially blokes his age. He wasn't one of the regulars."

"I see. Thank you."

She turned away and walked towards the bar at the other end of the room, which was staffed by a young woman with pink hair, styled in spikey bunches. She supposed the look was meant to be ironic, but to Prudence she just looked very young. This woman claimed she didn't recognise the picture either. She agreed with the other bartender's assessment that he wasn't a regular.

"I might have seen him."

Prudence whirled round to face a woman nearer her own age, with messy hair and a heavy metal T-shirt.

"Is he a lightweight, your son?"

"Why?"

"Because I think I remember him." She took a closer look at the picture, tilting her head one way, then the other.

Prudence didn't dare breathe. "When was this?"

"It must have been a good few weeks ago. He was staggering about a bit. My manager took his keys off him and handed them to his girlfriend."

Prudence exhaled. "Are you sure it was him?"

"Not a hundred percent, but he had a retro shirt on. U2, I think it was."

Prudence felt a tingle of excitement. "Yes, that's him!"

He'd been wearing that shirt the night he died. Instantly she was transported back to the garage, shaking his swollen body, trying to find a pulse.

"The girlfriend," she asked desperately. "What did she look like?"

"I don't remember anything about her."

Frantically, Prudence swiped through her pictures until she found one of Zoe.

"Is this her?"

"Sorry, I really don't remember."

"Okay. Thank you anyway. You've been a great help."

· · ·

PRUDENCE WALKED INTO THE OFFICE. The woman behind the desk stared at her with obvious distaste.

"Who let you in?"

Prudence leaned across the table. "My name is Prudence Ahern and I need to see your CCTV."

The woman cracked a smile. "You don't look like the old bill."

Prudence didn't smile back. "My son was murdered."

Her eyes widened. "Well, fuck. Why didn't you say?"

FIVE MINUTES LATER, Prudence was downstairs with the club's head of security.

"Can you show this lady CCTV footage from the night her son was in here?" the manager asked.

"Does she have a DPA Subject Access Request?" he asked.

"Why do I need one?"

"It's a legal requirement. To protect the patrons' privacy."

The manager let out a sigh. "How about you show her ... off the record?"

He drummed his fingers on the table. "Alright, but I'm not making any copies."

"Thank you," Prudence said.

He took her into another room and led her to a computer. "What night was it?"

"The twentieth. Last month."

Prudence trawled through hours of footage. It was very bad quality, all black and white and grainy. Most of the cameras were placed in the wrong locations, facing the tills and the dance floor. Her eyes drooped as she watched image after image. She saw a fight between two patrons, but neither of them was Nathan. She saw a girl puking in a corner and a couple sneaking into the disabled loos for a private rendezvous. She also saw the head of security shoving several people out of the club, but it wasn't her place to ask about that.

Then finally, she spotted him. The image was bad and the only thing she could see was Nathan walking into the men's toilets, and a few minutes later he walked out again. No, walking wasn't the word. He was staggering. That woman had been spot on. He looked drunk. She watched the rest of the footage, but she didn't get any more glimpses of him or the woman he was with.

She checked there was no one watching and then she recorded the images on her phone. This was evidence, and she wasn't prepared to part with it.

"I'm getting closer, Nathan," she told him.

But she wasn't close enough.

28

PRUDENCE

The sound of breaking glass shattered the peace, setting off all the neighbourhood dogs. Prudence ran to the window and saw the refuse collectors outside, tipping the recycling bins into their lorry. Damn, she'd forgotten to put hers out again.

She crawled back into bed but she didn't sleep for long. After a few more minutes, she gave up and made herself a cup of tea. Then she drifted back upstairs, coming to a halt outside Nathan and Zoe's room. She turned the handle and the door swung open with a creak. She didn't know what she'd expected to see but it was much the same as always. There were a few of Zoe's things here but not many. A hairbrush, a little bag of toiletries. A small number of clothes in the wardrobe. She still found it odd how few possessions Zoe owned.

She looked at the photos on the wall. There were several of Nathan and Bradley over the years. And there was the picture of him with Zoe and Bonnie on the day she was born. She was struck again by how sombre Zoe looked. Was she just exhausted from giving birth, or had she known what was to come? She gave a little sob. Zoe had lived under her roof for months and yet Prudence still had little idea who she was.

She shifted aside a pile of holiday brochures and found a book which appeared to be Nathan's diary.

"Bingo!"

She flicked desperately through the pages, but her excitement was short lived, as it appeared to be a functional sort of diary, with just dates and appointments. There was no mention of meeting a woman the night before he died. But, of course, if he was having an affair he wouldn't want Zoe to know about it, would he?

She flipped back and saw that Nathan had had an appointment with Steph at the student union, just a day after Bonnie was born. *What was that about?* she wondered. She recalled he had been struggling to keep up with his studies. Maybe he'd gone and asked for some sort of help.

Only one way to find out.

She drove over to the university. The student union building housed numerous cafés and bars on the ground floor, and on the upper floor there were meeting rooms and offices. She found a convenient noticeboard with pictures of all the staff, and studied Steph's picture. Could this be the woman her son had had an affair with? She looked a little old for him, and very different to Zoe, with closely cropped hair and thick glasses, but you never knew.

She located her office and knocked on her door.

"Hello? Can I help you?"

The woman looked just like her picture, except her hair had grown long enough to sit on her shoulders.

"Are you Steph?"

"That's what it says on the door."

Prudence took a step into her office. "I need to know what you talked to my son about."

Steph rose from her seat. "Oh! You must be Nathan's mum."

"How did you know?"

"He looked like you," Steph said.

She reached over and took both of Prudence's hands in hers. "Please, sit down."

Prudence pulled up a chair and waited anxiously as Steph got up and closed the door.

"Now, obviously I'm not supposed to give out the details of my meetings with the students, but in your case I'm willing to make an exception."

"And?"

"Nathan came to me because he wanted some legal advice. I'm not a lawyer, but we run a Citizens Advice service for the students, so I helped him as best I could. Specifically, he'd wanted to know how to take out an injunction against somebody."

Prudence exhaled. "Did he say who?"

Steph shook her head. "I'm afraid not."

"How can I find out if he managed to do it?"

Steph thought for a moment. "Well, he would have had to do so through a lawyer. I directed him to a website, but I don't know who he went with, if he even got that far."

"Did he ... did he say why he needed an injunction? What was it he needed to protect himself against?"

Steph took off her glasses and wiped them on her skirt. "Whatever it was, he was frightened. He said that he needed to do it soon. He didn't think it could wait."

RETURNING HOME, Prudence was struck once again by how still the house was. No dog, no Nathan, no Bonnie. Even Zoe's absence seemed strange somehow. She took the stairs straight up to Nathan's room and looked around for clues about the lawyer he might have spoken to. She hoped to find a business card or something, but there didn't appear to be anything like that lying around. Surely there had to be some papers or something, detailing what he'd done?

She walked over to the computer and shook the mouse to wake it up. She typed in Nathan's password. Thankfully he hadn't changed it. She found herself looking at his email account. She glanced at the list of emails, hoping to see one from his lawyer.

It took her a moment to realise that these were not Nathan's emails, but Zoe's. She felt a little guilty reading them but she needed this. She needed to understand what was going on.

Scrolling down, she found an email exchange between Zoe and Nathan. They were all sweet and pleasant, mostly written in the early days of their relationship. She skimmed Zoe's words briefly.

Ugh, this stuff was corny! She'd told him he was the yin to her yang. Nathan had written terrible emails too. His were not quite as slushy as Zoe's, but they were all in the same vein. Then, after the first couple of months, the emails took on a more serious tone. Zoe sounded frantic, frightened even, as she tried to gauge how Nathan felt:

Nathan,

If you are ever going to leave me then please, I'm begging you do it NOW! Because I swear if you wait until the baby's born, I don't think I can take it. I want whatever you want, baby or no baby. I just want what makes you happy,

Zoe xxx

Then came Nathan's reply:

Zoe,

What are you talking about? This is ridiculous. I would never dump you. Our love is far too powerful to ever be denied. I just think you should be the one to decide about the baby, that's all. It's your body after all. You must do whatever feels right to you. I love you like nothing on earth. Don't ever think I don't.

Nathan

Prudence sat back. This was the last one she could find. Why had Nathan and Zoe stopped emailing each other? It was so infuriating. If only they had continued, she might have had some idea of what had gone wrong. She checked Zoe's inbox again but there were no more emails between her and Nathan, not even in her archived messages. It looked as though Zoe had been emailing someone else regularly, though. *Ted Nithercott.* That had to be her dad.

She racked her brains. Had Zoe ever mentioned her dad? She didn't think so. On the contrary, she distinctly recalled Alana saying he was not in their lives. Perhaps she didn't know.

She opened one of the emails and read with interest, feeling a mixture of confusion and horror as she read Zoe's words. Old Prune, that was Zoe's name for her. She could have forgiven that. It was almost funny. But as she read on she discovered that each one was more disturbing than the last. Here in black and white was Zoe confessing to messing with her, hiding her towel and getting rid of her table.

She read the bit about Bob and felt a massive lump in her throat. So she had let him out! It seemed she felt bad about it.

As if that was any consolation. She kept reading, racing through Zoe's words.

She spoke in such riddles, it was hard to tell what she was getting at. What was it that worried her so much? Why did it matter if the baby was a boy or a girl? What was the significance? Prudence sat back and brushed the hair from her eyes. She must have been sitting reading for hours, but she was more confused than ever.

The cursor blinked at her, as if to say, 'What next?'

She thought for a moment, then typed in *Ted Nithercott*. He shouldn't be too hard to find with a name like that. She was right. There was only one Ted Nithercott on Facebook. She clicked on his profile page, then did a double take. *Ted Nithercott was dead.*

29

PRUDENCE

Prudence stared at the picture, trying to make out whether or not he looked like Zoe. She clearly took after Alana, with the exception of that chin. She looked closer. Yes, she thought she could see a likeness there.

She tilted back in her chair, trying to get her head round this new revelation. She went back to Zoe's emails. Her dad had not replied to a single one.

On his Facebook page, she found messages of condolence, dating back years. People posted to say they missed him on his birthday or on other special days. *How long had he been gone?*

One friend had posted on the anniversary of his death each year. There was something about the wording of the messages that made Prudence feel uneasy.

It never gets easier, mate.

Thinking of you again today.

Miss you, mate. The world is grim without you.

She clicked on the friend's profile. His name was Paul Barbour. She typed out a message to him, telling him about Nathan. She would have preferred to keep her son's name out of it. Typing those words was almost more painful than she could bear. But mentioning his death was likely to bring out compassion, and if she was going to get to the bottom of all this, she had to harness all the compassion she could get.

She laid down on Nathan's bed. She resisted the urge to return to the computer and hit the refresh button a couple of thousand times. Paul Barbour might be at work right now. She couldn't expect a response right away. Or he might not reply at all. Her message might just get swallowed up by his inbox. She closed her eyes and slept for a couple of hours. When she woke up, she went straight to the computer. Her spine tingled as she saw that Paul Barbour had replied.

Prudence, thank you for your message.

I'm sorry to hear about your loss. You asked about Ted and I'm afraid it's a very sad story. We worked together for a number of years. I always liked him. He was quiet and hardworking. More thoughtful than most of the people I've worked with. I suppose I was the closest to him of everyone in the company. Some of the others thought he was a bit weird, but he wasn't. He just enjoyed his job and liked to talk about it, even on the weekends. He was a family man, but he still volunteered for all the overtime he could get. For all our closeness, his death came as much of a surprise to me as it did to everyone else.

He wasn't ill as far as I know. I didn't think of him as anxious or depressed. He was introverted but I wouldn't have said he was particularly troubled. He had a stunning wife at home waiting for him. What did he have to be unhappy about? But the day he didn't turn up for work, I knew something was wrong because he was far too conscientious to take the day off for something minor, and not phoning in was unheard of. I called his home number but got no joy there, so in the end I contacted the police and they went round. Sadly, they found him in his garage, overcome by the fumes from his car.

Prudence pushed herself back from the table and ran full pelt into the bathroom. Her chest heaved as she vomited into the toilet over and over. She was certain now that Nathan hadn't killed himself. And nor had Ted Nithercott.

"So, you see, Zoe's father died in exactly the same way as Nathan. It can hardly be a coincidence, can it?"

Prudence folded her arms across her chest and waited expectantly.

PC Grainger looked at his superior.

The detective took a thoughtful slurp of his tea. "It could be a coincidence," he commented.

"Oh, come on!" Prudence wanted to ram his head into the wall.

Grainger furrowed his brow. On the phone it had sounded like he was on her side. But now he just sat there and said nothing, deferring to his boss.

The detective set his cup down. "Your daughter-in-law could have told your son how her dad died. Planted the idea in his head."

"No, there's more to it!"

"Do you know for sure that she didn't say something?"

"I never even heard her say anything about her dad. I didn't even know she had one."

Prudence thought about how Zoe had continued to write

to him. Did she even know he was dead? She wanted to mention it but then she'd have to admit she'd read Zoe's emails without her permission. That had to be against the law.

She peered into her own teacup. A thin layer of scum had formed across the surface. She pushed the cup away and concentrated on the police. "Are you at least going to look into it?"

She fixed her eyes on PC Grainger. He seemed like a meticulous chap, even if he had no backbone.

"We'll look into it," he said.

"Good."

The detective stood up from the table. "Let us know if you have any more thoughts. You know how to reach us."

Oh no, she wasn't letting him walk away that easily.

"When will I get an update?" she asked.

"We'll call you if there are any developments," Grainger said.

Prudence shook her head. "How about I call you? I'll give you a week."

Exhausted, Prudence returned home to stare at Ted Nithercott's Facebook page. She brought up his personal information. There was no mention of Zoe or Alana, but under the heading of 'family' a man called Jason Nithercott was listed as his son. Intrigued, she clicked on Jason's profile. Unfortunately, he had used a cartoon avatar instead of a real picture and there were no photos of him on the account.

All the same, there were a few details about him on the page. He lived alone, it appeared. No mention of friends or family. His page contained no clues about him at all, apart from a rather unnatural interest in leather. He was a member of a leather buy and sell group and had recently reviewed a new leather jacket.

She sent him a message asking him to contact her, then

went to make herself something to eat. Finding nothing in the cupboards, she reluctantly pulled one of Heidi's casseroles out of the freezer and stuck it in the microwave. Then she dashed back to the computer to see if he had replied. He hadn't.

Over dinner, she grew impatient. She trawled back through Jason's posts until she found one announcing that he'd got a new job at a café in Stoke on Trent. She glanced at the clock. If she left now, she could be there before closing time.

30

"Y ou sure that's the place you're looking for?" an older man asked, as Prudence locked her car.

"The Iron Horses?"

"Yes, that's it there."

There was a chill wind out and she fastened the buttons on her brown duffel coat.

"It's just I'm not sure you—"

His words were drowned out by the roar of Harley Davidsons as they zoomed into the car park, kicking up clouds of dust in their wake. She shrugged at the man and ventured onwards. She really hoped Jason was working tonight, after coming all this way. What a shame there was no phone number on his Facebook page. She missed the days when everyone was in the phone book. Life had been so much easier then.

THE CAFÉ WAS a little different to the way it had looked online. There were rows of motorbikes parked outside, and a group of petrolheads hung around admiring each other's bikes. Still, if Jason was in there, she was going to find him.

She took a step inside and looked around. Leather-clad men filled all the tables. There were some leather-clad women too, though not nearly as many. She had hoped to find Jason behind the counter but the man working there was too old to be him.

The group she'd seen outside were coming in now. They looked around and seemed miffed that there was nowhere to sit. They hung about, looking a bit awkward. There were a few looks exchanged between them and the occupants of the nearest table. She had a feeling that there was some history there.

One of the biker women came up to the counter to order. She was getting a lot of food and drinks for her table. The bartender turned round to pour the beers and one of the men who had just come in reached over and pinched her leather-clad bottom.

The room suddenly seemed hot. The next minute, the man who had taken the liberty was on the floor under the biker woman's boot. He got several sharp kicks of justice before he was allowed up and limped out of the café. Everyone carried on like nothing had happened.

Prudence approached the counter. "Excuse me," she said. "I'm looking for Jason."

"He's just gone on his break."

"When will he be back?"

The man gestured towards the door behind him. Prudence raised an eyebrow. "May I?"

"If you must."

She stepped behind the counter and pushed open the door. She found herself in a kitchen area with a kettle and microwave.

"Jason?" she called. She felt a blast of cold air down her back. A train rattled in the distance.

She heard the flush of a lavatory and a large, bearded man walked out. He was dressed in a similar style to the patrons, in a plain T-shirt and black leather jacket with various club badges on it.

He was looking at her. His blue eyes flashed dangerously – *but that chin.* There was no doubt he was Zoe's brother.

"I need to talk to you," she said. "It's about Zoe."

His eyes widened with surprise, but he gestured for her to follow him. They stepped into another room with a dining area. A plate of food sat on the table, along with utensils and mustard.

"You don't mind if I eat my dinner, do you?" he asked.

"No, of course not."

"What's this about then?"

He stabbed a potato with his fork and brought it to his mouth.

"I'm Zoe's ... well, I suppose you could call me her mother-in-law."

He sat up straight. "I didn't know she was married."

"She wasn't. My son Nathan, he was Bonnie's dad."

He shook his head. "Sorry, you've lost me. Who's Bonnie?"

"Zoe's daughter."

Jason's mouth opened, still full of potato. Clearly, he needed a minute to take this in. She looked through her phone and brought up the picture of them on the day Bonnie was born. His eyes flickered over the picture, and he pressed a finger to her phone to enlarge it.

"I didn't know she'd even left home," he said, shaking his head.

"Zoe went to Loughborough University. To study finance."

He smiled. "Yeah, that sounds about right."

"That's where she met my son, Nathan. They were smitten with each other. She quickly fell pregnant and had Bonnie. Soon afterwards, Nathan died. That was just over a month ago."

She felt a lump in her throat, but she pushed on through the tears. "I don't know what happened, but then I discovered your dad also died in similar circumstances."

Jason dropped his fork. "Fuck."

She waited a moment as he absorbed this information. He kept shaking his head.

"I came here today because I'm trying to find out what happened. I wondered if there was anything you could tell me? I know very little about your sister, really. And she's taken Bonnie and gone back to live with your mum now, so I don't know where to turn."

Jason stopped eating. His Adam's apple bobbed. "I think I can give you some insight."

He drew in a large breath, and began speaking.

"When I was little, I was very close to my mum. I loved my dad too, but my mum was my world. I had a beautiful bedroom, which Mum painted pink. It was filled with dolls and frilly things. This may sound odd to you," he said, as he gestured to his now very masculine appearance, "but I didn't know any different and I was perfectly happy. I had long hair, and I mean, really long, down to my waist. Mum used to love playing with it and plaiting it. But when I was about seven, some of the kids at school made fun of me and told me I looked like a girl, so I got hold of some scissors and cut it all off. When Mum saw what I'd done, she was hysterical. She told me I was evil and that she hated me. I told her it was just hair and it would grow back but she didn't want to know. She stopped loving me just like that."

His nostrils flared and his lips curled into a bitter half smile.

"Within a year, my sister was born. Mum made me move

out of the pretty pink room into the box room with all the junk. My baby sister was now the apple of her eye and I hated her for it, although Dad tried hard to explain to me that it was not Zoe's fault. She was just an innocent baby. Mum had pulled me out of school after I cut my hair and we switched to home schooling. Zoe and I were both educated according to Mum's whims. We rarely mixed with other children and led a sheltered life, which did little to prepare us for the outside world. My dad had a good heart, but I wish he could have found the strength to stand up to her but he never did.

"I tried to make it up to Mum. I grew my hair long again and tried to be the person she wanted, but it didn't work. I was always doing things to please her. I would help her with the housework without even being asked and I tried to anticipate her moods. I'd put her slippers out, for when she finished work. I'd put her favourite music on and bring her glasses of wine, but nothing I did was ever good enough. Mum treated me like a second-class citizen, deliberately giving me less food than Zoe, even though I was older. She was forever punishing me for the slightest thing, whilst Zoe could do no wrong.

"Eventually, I stopped trying. There were no real patterns to her behaviour. No reason why one day I could eat with the rest of the family at the table, and the next I wasn't even allowed out of my room.

"As for Dad, he died when I was sixteen. I don't know exactly what happened. I thought at the time that Mum had driven him to suicide. She told us he had left but I could tell she was lying, so I decided to run away. I asked Zoe to come too, but she told on me. It was weeks before I was able to get another chance."

He looked down at his cracked knuckles. He was a full-grown man with tattoos and a beard, but she saw the lost little boy that he once was and she wanted to wrap her arms around him and hug him.

She suspected he was still bitter about the way Zoe had betrayed him. But she could see now that if Zoe acted strange, it was because of her unorthodox upbringing. Zoe's mother had poisoned her against Jason, and indeed against men. It was a miracle she had still managed to find love with Nathan.

"That must have been awful for you," she said. "Have you really not seen Zoe in all these years? She's in a really tough place right now, back with your mother. I get the feeling she doesn't want to be there, that she feels she has no choice. Your mum is smitten with the baby, Bonnie, but Zoe isn't coping at all. I think your mother is suffocating her, emotionally. If you have it in you, I really think you should reach out and speak to Zoe. She needs your support more than ever."

Jason didn't look convinced, but she scribbled down Zoe's number for him.

"Thank you for talking to me," she said, as she left.

"Wait!" he scribbled something down on a piece of paper and slid it across to her. "That's my mobile number. Just in case."

"Thank you." She slipped it into her pocket.

She nodded to the bartender as she made her way out of the café. One of the bikers held the door for her as she walked out to her car. She sank into the driver's seat, still processing what Jason had told her. What a messed-up childhood he'd had, living with a mother who wanted him to be a girl. That must have totally screwed with his head.

It was getting late now, and she had a fair way to drive. She headed out on to the roundabout but at the last minute she changed her mind and turned right instead of left. There was a honking of horns and she raised her hand in apology, then headed in the opposite direction to the one she had come from.

"I'm coming, Zoe," she whispered, as she drove through the night.

Russet Way was silent, dark except for the glow of porch lights that flickered intermittently on and off. Prudence killed her engine and waited. She'd parked in a space a little way round the circle of houses. She hoped Alana wouldn't spot her car there, hidden as it was by the leaves of a large oak.

She closed her eyes and tried to let the sleep wash over her. There was too much adrenaline in her veins and her brain was buzzing with everything she'd learned, trying to put it all together. But if she didn't sleep now, she didn't know when she would.

When the sun came up she was cold and thirsty. It hadn't occurred to her to stop off and shop for provisions, though she had passed a garage less than a mile down the street. She thought about doing so now, but she couldn't risk missing Alana. She was banking on her going to work today. She needed to get Zoe alone.

She watched the house for some time before she was finally rewarded. Alana strolled out in one of her crisp linen suits and climbed into yet another new car, this time a silver Mazda. Prudence waited until she drove out of the cul-de-sac before she ventured out of her car. The grass verge was damp with morning dew as she hurried across it, and she could already hear Bonnie's cries.

31

Bonnie's wails grew louder as Zoe opened the door.

Zoe's hair was matted and had lost all its shine. Her clothes were baggy and creased. Her eyelids were heavy and her top was stained. As for Bonnie, she was bending backwards in Zoe's arms, wailing and shrieking, trying to wriggle free. Before Prudence could say a word, Zoe plonked the baby in her arms and retreated into the house. Prudence followed her inside.

Her first concern was for Bonnie. Her nappy was so heavy it was coming apart.

"Where are the clean nappies?" she asked.

Zoe pointed upwards. Prudence carried Bonnie up the stairs, and instinctively took a left, where she found the famed pink nursery. It was as beautiful as she had imagined, with everything a baby could need. The toys sat neatly on the shelf. There was a window seat, looking out at the circle and a rainbow mobile that was straight out of a style magazine.

She headed for the changing table and laid Bonnie down, quickly locating everything she needed. Bonnie kept on crying as the cold air hit her legs. Prudence changed her nappy and replaced her fussy outfit with a simple pink Baby-gro, but still she didn't calm down.

"What's wrong? Are you hungry?"

She brought Bonnie downstairs to the kitchen, where she found an elaborate machine for warming the formula. She jiggled Bonnie in her arms while she waited. It was a very nice kitchen, full of fancy gadgets, including a state-of-the-art cappuccino maker, a bread maker and a large food processor. All of this surprised Prudence, as she hadn't pictured Alana doing much in the kitchen. But then again, maybe she didn't. She seemed like someone who liked to chase shiny new objects. She was probably more interested in owning all these things than actually using them.

The machine beeped. Prudence took out the warm bottle of milk, then took Bonnie into the lounge. Zoe had curled up on the sofa, her head resting on a cushion. She looked utterly miserable and exhausted.

Prudence settled herself down in the armchair and posi-tioned Bonnie on her lap. She took her milk instantly, grip-ping the bottle with both hands as she sucked it down.

"How are you?" she asked Zoe.

"Tired," Zoe said. "I never knew it would be so exhausting."

"Hasn't your mum been helping you?"

"Yes, of course. Mum's great with babies. She's ..."

"Working full time?" Prudence supplied.

Zoe nodded.

Prudence shifted her position. "You don't look like you're getting much sleep."

"What's sleep?"

Prudence drew a breath. "It doesn't sound like this arrangement is working too well for you."

Zoe pressed her lips together. "It's fine. We're fine. You just ... caught me on a bad day."

"Have there been many good days?"

"How can there? Without Nathan ..."

Bonnie had drunk all the way down to the bottom of the bottle. Prudence placed the baby over her shoulder and rubbed her back to aid digestion.

Zoe looked at her resentfully. "If only she'd been a boy, she'd have had such a great life."

"Because your mum wouldn't want her?"

Zoe looked down at her hands. She was clearly struggling to speak out against Alana.

"Have you remembered to take your antidepressants?"

Zoe shrugged, like there was no longer any point.

"They'll help you feel better," she said softly. Bonnie's eyelids were fluttering. Prudence should really put her down, but she wanted to hold her a little longer and take in that delicious baby smell. She had missed her so much.

"Why don't you come home with me? I can help you with Bonnie. Your mum can visit as much as she wants. I know she wants to be in Bonnie's life too, but we can work something out. Maybe she could have her on alternate weekends."

At that moment she would have said anything to change Zoe's mind.

"It's not that simple."

"Isn't it?"

They sat in silence for a while. "You loved Nathan, didn't you, Zoe?"

Zoe's eyes filled with tears. "Of course, I did."

"You do know that he died in the exact same way as your dad?"

Zoe jumped to her feet. Her face was bright red. "You have to leave now!"

She wrenched the sleeping baby from Prudence's arms. Prudence wanted to resist, but she didn't want to disturb Bonnie.

"My dad is not dead and you have to leave," Zoe repeated. She looked a little frenzied now. Her eyes were angry, filled with spite.

Prudence hauled herself to her feet. She took a few steps towards the door, then stopped.

"Your mum needs help, Zoe. I know she kept the truth from you. That's why you were never able to accept your dad's death."

Zoe's eyes blazed with fury. "I told you, he's not dead. He just left."

"I talked to Jason, Zoe, and he told me everything."

Zoe gave a bitter laugh. "You can't believe anything he says. Jason is no good."

"You must know your dad is dead. He never responded to any of your emails."

"Who the hell do you think you are, reading my emails?" Zoe shoved her with one hand, causing Bonnie to stir and howl. Prudence wanted to stand her ground, but she could see that Zoe was upset. Reluctantly, she walked down the hall and out onto the front step.

The door slammed loudly behind her.

32

Prudence stood on the doorstep, debating what to do. A part of her wanted to march back in there and take Bonnie. Or perhaps she should call social services because Zoe clearly wasn't coping. She drew a deep breath. No, Zoe needed time to process what she had said. It wasn't easy, but she was going to have to let her deal with this. She had to leave. For now.

She drove home on auto pilot, her conversations with Jason and Zoe playing in her head. There was no real way of knowing if what Jason had told her was the truth, but it felt right. Zoe was deeply unhappy living with her mum, and she didn't feel like she could leave. And that fear wasn't just in Zoe's head. There was a very real possibility that Alana was a stone-cold killer.

She rang Jason when she got home and told him about her visit. "I'm begging you, speak to Zoe. Maybe you can convince her of the truth."

Jason was silent for a moment. "I can try but I doubt she'll listen to me. She never has."

Prudence rubbed her eyes. "I think she's beginning to

crack," she told him. "She might be more open to the truth
than ever before."

PRUDENCE MADE herself some tea and toast, then went to bed
for a couple of hours. When she woke, she had a missed call
from Jason. She called him back.

"I talked to Zoe like you asked," he told her.

"How did it go? Do you think you got through to her?"

"Hard to say. I really don't understand how she could not
know about Dad's death. She only had to look him up."

"I'm sure on some level she's aware of that. Perhaps she
wasn't ready to face the truth."

The rest of the day passed in a blur. Prudence spoke with
a lawyer friend about getting access to Bonnie, but he wasn't
terribly optimistic.

"I think you have a good case but it will take you time and
money, and even then, there's no guarantee you'll win.
Grandparents' rights are not well protected in law."

"But I'm the one who's cared for her since she was born.
Surely that must carry some weight? If Bonnie could speak,
she would ask to be with me. I'm certain of it."

"I hear what you're saying, but it could be hard to prove in
court if your daughter-in-law doesn't back you up. Do you
think she would?"

Prudence let out a big sigh. "No," she replied. "Probably
not."

DESPITE HER BEST INTENTIONS, she didn't make it to bed until
the early hours, and then she tossed and turned, running the
gauntlet of her dreams. Often, she woke up drenched in
sweat, haunted by fragmented memories. This one was pleasant, though. She clung onto it and her brain flooded with a

memory of running through a forest, chasing Bob. He turned and looked at her with his big goofy grin and she reached out and stroked his rug-like fur. She smiled to herself and shut her eyes again. Then her body stiffened. She thought she heard a scratching sound.

She lay still and listened. There it was: *scrape, scrape, scrape.* Softly, she climbed out of bed and tiptoed across the room. Light spilled across the landing from Nathan and Zoe's room. She must have left the light on. Or had she? She picked up a hefty Hilary Mantel book from her bedside table and stole across the landing. She also reached for her cordless phone and popped it into her dressing gown pocket, just in case. She burst into Nathan's room and looked around. There was nothing unusual, except ... the corner of the duvet was folded back. Had she left it like that? She couldn't be sure. She sank to her knees, inspecting the bed underneath. Nothing there. She scuttled over to the wardrobe and threw open the doors. Nothing. Only darkness, the windows filled with shadows. Then she heard a fluttering sound and her heart leapt into her mouth. Under Nathan's desk was a holiday brochure and the pages were turning one by one. She picked it up and placed it back on the desk.

Just the wind, she told herself. The corner of one of the pages had been folded back. She looked at a picture of Mount Cook. It looked beautiful. Maybe she would go there sometime.

She walked back out onto the landing. There it was again: *scratch, scratch, scratch.* Could there be someone downstairs? She stood completely still. The house quietened with her. Even the radiators stopped whining.

She longed to go back to bed, but there was no way she could sleep until she investigated. She flicked on the light and took a couple of steps down the stairs. *Scratch, scratch, scratch.* Another step. Her eyes swept the room below. The light swung gently from the lampshade. She placed her foot on the next step and it gave way as though it was rotten.

Her arms windmilled frantically as she tried to regain her balance. The Hilary Mantel book thudded down the stairs and she toppled after it, catching the banister halfway down.

"Ow!"

She sank down on the middle stair, clutching the banister with her right hand. She'd knocked her knee, but other than that she seemed to be alright. She listened intently, but whatever it was had fallen silent. She pulled herself to her feet and collected her book at the bottom. She walked through to the kitchen and poured herself a glass of water. Then thought better of it and had a sherry. She picked up the vegetable knife and slipped it into her dressing gown pocket, then she marched around her house, checking every door and every window. They all appeared to be closed. There was only one place she hadn't checked and that was the garage. Unfortunately, that was the one place her frazzled nerves wouldn't let her go.

She retreated to bed and pulled the covers over her head. When she awoke, her neck was stiff and her shoulders were full of tension. There was a dull ache in her right knee too. She must have twisted it in her midnight fall.

She got up and walked to the top of the stairs again, kneeling to examine the step she'd fallen on. The stair tread had come loose.. And it hadn't ever been before.

Heidi rang and they agreed they would meet at the café in the park. Then Prudence locked herself in the bathroom and took a long shower. She could call the police, but would they even come? And if they did, would they even find anything? She was starting to wonder if she should go away for a few nights just to get a bit of peace.

The phone rang again just as she was getting out of the shower. She grabbed a towel and rubbed herself down briskly, then hurried back to her bedroom. She glanced down at the display then froze as she saw the number. It was Alana. The ringing stopped.

What did Alana want? Or could it be Zoe, ringing from her mum's phone? She grabbed some clothes from her drawer: underwear, T-shirt, jogging bottoms and pulled it all on. The phone started up again. *Brring, brring.* Was it always this loud?

She reached for the receiver and brought it to her ear.

"Hello?"

A loud, high-pitched scream echoed down the phone. She drew back, switching it to loudspeaker. She should record this. If only she had her mobile, but she'd left it downstairs in the kitchen to charge. She waited for Alana – and it was definitely Alana – to stop her hysterics, but before she could get a word in Alana was ranting at her, threatening her with a stream of foul language. Her voice sounded anguished and hurt.

"Leave us alone. Stay out of our lives or I'll call the police on you. You're not allowed anywhere near Bonnie, do you hear me? Stop messing with Zoe. How dare you fuck with her head like that? You're a sad, lonely old loser, you know that? How dare you drag Jason into this? He's not part of our family. He's not anything."

Prudence cleared her throat. "Excuse me, but I think you'll find—"

Alana's voice dropped to a low, deep rumble. "Get this through your thick head: you had Bonnie for long enough. Now it's my turn and I need you to back off, if you know what's good for you."

"What's good for—"

Alana cut through her words with a loud, obnoxious laugh.

Prudence put down the phone. One thing was clear. That woman was not well.

She ran a hand through her damp hair. She couldn't be bothered to dry it. She needed to leave to meet Heidi soon. She'd tell her what was going on. She'd know what to do.

She wrapped a silk scarf around her neck and put her coat and shoes on, then reached for her handbag. The postman met her at the door.

"Good morning."

"Morning." He smiled as he handed her two thick envelopes.

Prudence took them and carried them back into the house to look at later. She saw that the top one was addressed to Bonnie. She looked at the other. It was for Zoe.

She tore open Bonnie's and found herself looking at a brand-new passport. She hadn't even known Zoe had applied for one. It had one of the new blue covers. She opened it up and looked at the picture. Bonnie must only be days old here. Her cheeks were still a little bloated and she had tired, sleepy eyes. Judging from the size of the other envelope, it must be a passport for Zoe. Had she been planning a holiday of some kind? She'd never mentioned it.

As she walked out to her car, she felt a prickle of apprehension. She still had that creepy feeling, as if someone was watching her, but she couldn't see anyone except the neighbourhood tom. He had been getting more brazen since Bob had died. Perhaps he had found a way into her house last night. Perhaps he'd even got into the garage. That wouldn't explain the loose stair tread, though. Surely a cat couldn't cause that much damage.

Heidi was already at the café. She smiled and waved as Prudence approached. Then another woman stepped into her path.

"Prudence! How are you? You're looking very trim. Retirement must agree with you!"

Prudence blinked. It took her a moment to place the woman, a young nurse she'd worked with a while ago.

"God, I envy you," her former colleague went on. "I bet you get to lie in as long as you want in the mornings now!"

Prudence fought for an appropriate response.

"I ... er ..."

"And I bet you don't miss the paperwork!"

The woman chuckled and Prudence offered her a weak smile, then darted away before she became entangled in a longer conversation. She sank down at Heidi's table and picked up the menu, even though she already knew it by heart.

"She must not have heard," Heidi said.

"No."

She thought of all the wonderful plans she'd had for her retirement. The endless days out in the garden. The walks she would take with Bob. She could never have imagined it would end up like this, not in a million years.

A moment later, the waitress came over and placed a latte in front of Prudence.

"I ordered for you," Heidi said.

"Thanks." As Prudence leaned forward to take a sip, a shiver went up her back.

"What's wrong?" Heidi asked.

"Nothing. Just had a bad night."

She angled her chair slightly to the left, so that she could see people coming in and out. Her throat still felt dry. She heard a rustle behind her. She turned to look but there was no one there, just an old paper bag blowing about. When she turned back, Heidi was looking at her with concern.

She told her about the night she'd had. Heidi looked aghast.

"You have to get that stair fixed. I know a man who's really good."

Prudence gritted her teeth. "The broken stair isn't the point. I think it was Alana. I think she broke into my house and messed with it."

Heidi's face twitched. "You think?"

"Look, I know this sounds far-fetched but hear me out. There was a scratching sound, like Bob used to make, and then the stair was broken. I've never had a problem with that stair before. And I think someone turned the light on in Nathan's room."

"Did you actually see anyone?"

"No."

"How would she even have got in?"

Prudence thought for a moment. "She could have used Zoe's key."

Heidi sat up straighter. "I'm not sure about Alana breaking in, but you should change the lock, just in case."

"It was definitely Alana."

"How can you be so certain?"

"Because she called me this morning and started ranting and raving down the phone."

"You're kidding? Why?"

"Probably because I contacted her estranged son. I got him to call Zoe. I was hoping he could talk some sense into her."

Heidi set down her cup. "I suppose from her point of view she might have thought you were meddling?"

"Meddling?" Prudence would have laughed, but it wasn't the least bit funny. She gulped down her latte and wedged a ten-pound note under her cup. "You're not taking me seriously. I mean it, Heidi. I think that woman is out to get me."

She stood up and pushed the table back.

"Pru, don't be like that!"

"I'm not being like anything. I'm just ... really tired. Let's talk about this another time, okay?"

"Okay." Heidi's eyes were sad as Prudence left the table, but she couldn't help it. She wasn't in the mood to argue.

When she reached her car, Prudence called the locksmith and arranged to meet him at her house at six o'clock that evening. She didn't much feel like returning home, not until the locks were changed. She should have just swallowed her pride and gone over to Heidi's but she was still cross, so she went to the cinema instead. Before Zoe came along, she and Nathan had gone there frequently. They never missed a Bond film and there was a new one out that week. She needed to catch up.

She went in and bought her ticket, then joined the queue for popcorn.

"Do want the regular or the large?" the woman behind the counter asked with a bored expression.

"I don't know, what do you think?" Prudence turned to her left, then realised with a start that Nathan wasn't there.

"I think you should get whatever you want," the woman said.

"Er, no. Sorry, I've changed my mind."

She took a step backwards, almost colliding with the man behind her. Then she turned on her heel and hurried out, past the ticket counter and outside into the street, where she gulped down great lungfuls of air. She felt as though she'd just run a marathon, but it was all in her head. At that moment, she missed Nathan so badly it hurt. A powerful wave of pain threatened to pull her under but she kept walking, putting one foot in front of the other, until she reached her car.

She drove to Morrisons and got herself a trolley. She found it comforting, pushing it up and down the aisles. She remembered seeing Nathan when he worked here, running into him unexpectedly as he was stacking the shelves. He was always happy to see her. He'd never gone through that embarrassed phase that some people's kids went through. She didn't feel much like cooking so she grabbed items that were easy to prepare, like noodles and soup.

"Prudence!"

She whirled round and found herself facing Caroline.

"I've missed seeing you at Zumba."

"Yes, well ..."

Caroline took in the contents of Prudence's trolley. Prudence resented the pity in her eyes.

"I'm cooking paella tonight," Caroline said. "Why don't you join us? There'll be wine."

"Thanks," she said. "Maybe another time. I just need to ..." What did she need to do exactly? The word she was looking for was probably 'wallow'.

Caroline nodded vigorously. "Of course, I understand. You let me know whenever you feel like doing things again. I'm always here. So is Jackie."

Prudence nodded. She couldn't tell her how hard it was to catch up with old friends. She couldn't say how jealous she was to hear about their perfectly healthy children. She even envied Jackie's tearaway son, who had been arrested more than a few times over the past few years. At that moment, she would have given anything for a call from the police station, asking to bail Nathan out. Not that Nathan had ever done anything like that. He had been a good person, everybody said so. It was so unfair that he was gone, while everyone else was still here.

Instinctively, Caroline reached forward. She gave Prudence a hug so big it almost knocked her off her feet. To her horror, tears sprang to her eyes.

"Sorry!" Caroline said. "I didn't mean to upset you."

Prudence wiped the tears away. "No, you haven't. Thank you. That was just what I needed."

They said goodbye and Prudence resumed her shopping as if nothing had happened. Would it ever feel normal, she wondered. Or would her whole life be like this from now on?

By the time she'd loaded her shopping into the boot of her car, she was running late. She nudged the little car to go faster. The road ahead was clear, so she wasn't hurting anyone. Most people exceeded the speed limit anyway. It was only people like her who—

She heard a car behind her and glimpsed bright head-lights in her mirror. Seconds later, she felt the impact. Her head hit the back of her seat and she bit down hard on her tongue. Her wheels spun like crazy. She stamped on the brakes, but she no longer had control of the car. She braced herself as she left the road at speed. Her foot slipped off the pedals. The last thing she remembered was the roar of an engine as the other car sped off.

33

PRUDENCE

Prudence felt distant, weightless, as if she was floating through space. She might have continued to stare into the nothingness if it weren't for the persistent drip, drip, drip on her shoulder. Something was leaking. Something cold and wet. Was that blood? The smell was intoxicating. Powerful, light and woody. It gave her a flash of memories too fleeting to hold on to. That was it, it was petrol. The car was leaking petrol. She was going to die. Good.

She closed her eyes and tried to get comfy. Her seatbelt felt too tight across her chest. Pain throbbed in her neck and shoulders. She ignored it. She was floating again, enjoying that pleasant weightless feeling.

"Mum!" She heard Nathan's voice clear as day. "Mum! You've got to get out."

She opened her eyes. She was hanging upside down. She took a deep breath. And another. That was good. Now, she needed to cut the engine.

She reached forward. Her eyes stung as she found the controls. It was getting smoky. Where was her phone? She patted her pockets, but it wasn't there. She'd left it in her handbag but where was that? She reached up to touch the ceiling. Her shoulder screamed in protest but she kept going. Using her other hand, she fumbled for her seatbelt

Her fingers shook as she found the release. She jolted forwards. Her shoulder screamed with pain. She reached for the door handle and rattled it. It was jammed. The petrol smell was getting stronger now. She was going to have to crawl across to the other door.

The car was an oven. Her eyes watered, blurring her vision. She squirmed around to find the right way to move. She wasn't used to doing things at this angle, and her injured shoulder was making itself known in sharp, painful spasms.

She found the other door and tried the handle. It held firm. She moved up and pressed her weight against it. All at once, the door flew open and she fell out of the car. Pain exploded in her shoulder. She held it tight, moaning as fresh spasms rocketed through her.

Slowly, she turned her head. The car was smouldering now. The windows were all misted up and the smell was unbearable. She scrambled to her feet and tripped over the straps of her bag, which had tumbled out with her. She grabbed the handles and staggered unevenly down the hill. She was ten feet away when she heard the explosion.

She turned and watched as her car transformed into a raging fireball. She knew she should keep going but her exhausted body wouldn't cooperate. She collapsed in a heap as the thick black smoke filled the air.

34

P rudence opened her eyes. Her vision was blurred, and it took her a moment to focus. Her lips felt dry and sticky, and her tongue had become a razor. She had a flash of rolling over and over in her car. *Was she in hospital?* She tried to lift her head.

"Prudence! You're awake!"

Zoe's face drifted into her vision. Her dark eyes were round and watery.

Prudence blinked. "What ... what are you doing here?"

"I got a call on Nathan's phone because he was your next of kin. Oh god, Prudence, I was so worried!"

She got a whiff of apple and honey blossom. Someone was holding her other hand. She turned her head and her eyes met Alana's. Her make-up was as pristine as ever but she was missing all expression. Not smiling, not glaring, not ... anything. It was like staring into the eyes of a dead person. Utterly chilling and yet almost impossible to look away.

"Get away from me!" she rasped. Alana smiled slowly. She was blocking the cord, so Prudence couldn't reach it to alert the staff.

"Help!" Prudence called, trying to get the attention of a nurse but her voice came out as a rasp.

Alana leaned closer, one hand resting on her pillow. There was a bright red gash on her hand.

"I don't understand what happened?" Zoe said. "Were you speeding? They said you rolled into a ditch?"

"A car rammed me off the road," Prudence whispered.

"Oh, Prudence, that's awful!"

She rubbed her throat. "It was a silver Mazda." She wasn't at all certain of this, but that was the last car she'd seen Alana driving.

Zoe's eyes widened, suggesting she recognised this description, but Alana didn't flicker. Prudence was still looking around, trying to get the attention of the staff. A nurse finally materialised and Prudence waved frantically.

For goodness' sake, do your job, she silently chastised the woman.

The nurse's face grew stern. She looked from Zoe to Alana. "How did you get in here? Miss Ahern is not ready for visitors."

Alana smiled sweetly. "Oh, but your colleague said—"

"Well, I'm in charge and I'm telling you it's time to leave. Visiting hours are on the door."

"Just a few more minutes," Alana pleaded, but the nurse shook her head.

"You can come back at visiting time," she said firmly.

To Prudence's relief, Alana actually made for the door. Zoe made an apologetic face and trailed after her.

The nurse turned back to Prudence. "How are you feeling? You've had a very long sleep."

"Closer!" Prudence rasped, beckoning with her fingers.

The nurse leaned in so she could hear.

"I need you to call the police. That woman is extremely

dangerous. Her name is Alana Nithercott and she's the one who caused my accident. I think she wants to kill me."

The nurse blinked. *She thought she was nuts. Of course, she did.* Prudence had been in her position many times before.

"This is for real," she said, wishing she wasn't so weak. "If you don't do something, she will come back and finish me off. Call the police and alert security. Please, hurry."

The nurse hesitated for a moment, then jogged out of the room. Prudence wasn't sure if she was following her instructions or if she'd gone to get the doctor. She returned a few minutes later.

"Don't worry," she said. "Those women are being escorted off the premises. Now I really need to check how you're doing." She took out a digital thermometer.

"I don't have a temperature," Prudence protested. "Believe me, I was a nurse."

"I still need to check."

Prudence nodded.

"There. You're quite right, it's normal."

"Good."

Prudence's eyes darted to the door. She didn't have a good view of it. She tried to shift her weight but her shoulder objected. "Ow!"

"Try to rest," the nurse said gently. "I've paged the doctor for you. He ought to be here soon. Now, I need to take some blood. Which vein do you think I should go for?"

At that moment, the doctor walked in. He was a tall man, with a slightly self-satisfied air but Prudence was just glad it wasn't someone she knew.

"Hi, Prudence," he greeted her. "I must say you're looking better already."

Prudence furrowed her brow. "Have we met?"

"Indeed we have, but you were in and out of it for a while there. Are you in any pain?"

"My shoulder hurts like a bitch."

"Okay, we might need to top up your pain meds. I don't think you've broken anything, but I'd like to send you for some X-rays just to be sure."

She nodded.

"Okay, I'll arrange for someone to come up and get you. It'll be about twenty minutes, okay?"

Prudence nodded and wondered how long it would really take.

BY THE TIME she returned from the X-ray, the food trolleys were doing the rounds. Her friendly but talkative porter helped her back into bed and a tray was placed in front of her. Her stomach rumbled. She couldn't remember when she had last eaten.

"Oh, isn't that nice?" the porter said. "Someone's sent you some flowers! I do love sweet williams."

He leaned over to sniff them.

"Stop!" she cried. "I wouldn't touch those if I were you!"

He turned and looked at her oddly.

"No one knows I'm here," she clarified. "Except Alana and Zoe. Alana is the one who tried to kill me. That woman is dangerous. She—"

"Alright, I get the picture."

He leaned over and picked up the vase.

"Make sure you throw them outside," Prudence told him. "She might have laced them with poison or something. She's a very disturbed woman."

The porter nodded and scuttled off. She watched him with concern. She hoped he heeded her words.

She investigated her food tray and wolfed down a bowl of something that might have been soup but could equally have been curry or stew – it was hard to tell from the consistency – then she drank a cup of tea.

ONCE HER TRAY had been collected, she settled herself back against the pillows. Other patients on the ward were watching TV or trying to sleep but Prudence didn't want to get distracted. She kept a constant lookout, one eye on the staff, the other on the door.

Not long after, a doctor came to see her. A different one this time. He had a nice bedside manner.

"I'd like to keep you in for observation," he told her. "We need to make sure you don't have a serious head injury. I want to keep an eye on your blood pressure, too. It's a little high."

There's a surprise.

"The good news is that your X-rays look good. No broken bones. Your shoulder will be painful for a while, but we'll keep you topped up with painkillers to help with that. You were lucky, Prudence. Incredibly lucky."

DESPITE HER BEST INTENTIONS, Prudence dropped off to sleep. She woke up to find Heidi sitting beside her. Heidi's brow was heavy, and her jaw looked tense.

Prudence flashed her a smile. "Finally! What took you so long?"

"It's not funny. You could have died."

"You think I don't know that?"

Heidi shook her head. "I can't lose you, Pru," she said fiercely. "You've got to take better care of yourself."

"I'm trying!"

"Is there anything I can do for you?"

"Yes, I need you to call the locksmith. I was due to meet

him at my house last night. He must be wondering why I didn't turn up."

"I'm sure he'll understand, given the circumstances! What happened? Zoe said you were in a car accident."

Prudence reeled back. "When did you speak to Zoe?"

"She called me."

"How did she get your number?"

"I gave it to her a while ago."

"Why? You barely know her."

"I wanted to help her. I could see how cut up she was after … you know."

Prudence rubbed her arm. It was just like Heidi to look out for Zoe, but she still felt funny about it. Why hadn't she said anything at the time?

She filled Heidi in on the details of her accident, at least as far as she was able to remember. "I think it was Alana, trying to run me down," she concluded.

"Did you actually see her face?" Heidi asked.

"No, but she came here with Zoe to gloat."

"Are you sure? Zoe probably needed a lift. She doesn't drive, does she?"

Prudence took a deep breath and willed herself not to scream. "I really need to speak to the police," she said. "So much has happened in the last couple of days. I really think I need to—"

"The police already came and went," Heidi told her. "The nurse mentioned it. She said you were asleep."

"Why didn't they wake me?"

"They probably thought you needed your rest, and you do. You look like you've been dragged through a hedge backwards."

"Cheers."

"I mean it, Pru. You need to take it easy and stop coming up with all these conspiracy theories."

"For god's sake, Heidi. Alana is trying to kill me!"

"It just seems so incredible."

"Look, believe what you want, but I need you to hang around. I think Alana might come back tonight, and I don't want to have to face her on my own. If you could spend the night, I'd feel a lot safer."

Heidi looked perplexed. "You know I'd do anything for you, but I don't think they'll let me stay, Pru. I have to be out of here as soon as visiting hours are up."

"Just hang around," Prudence begged. "You can sit out there in the waiting room. I've seen people do it loads of times."

For a moment, she thought Heidi was going to refuse, but then she nodded abruptly.

"Alright then. If it makes you feel safer." She reached for Prudence's hand and squeezed it.

"What would I do without you?" Prudence asked.

"Do try to sleep," said the nurse, when she came to top up Prudence's pain meds. The rest of the ward was settling down for the night, but the quieter it grew, the more alarmed she felt. How could she possibly sleep? She was a sitting duck.

She lay propped up in bed, her eyes and ears alert to the faintest sound, the slightest movement. Shoes squeaked as the nurses went on their rounds. Machines beeped throughout the night, and sometimes she heard loud whispered conversations. Occasionally, she nodded off, but each time she jerked awake, the pain in her shoulder reminding her that she was still here. She was still alive. She swept the ward with her eyes, taking in every shadow. Alana would be back; she was sure of it. And this time she might not be so lucky.

At some point in the early hours, she lost her fight and

fell into a deep, troubled sleep. She awoke to find a tall figure standing over her, holding a needle. She let out a loud, blood-curdling scream.

"It's okay!" a voice hushed her. "It's just me."

Prudence blinked. It was just a nurse. A student nurse: she remembered working with him once or twice. He had been keen but clumsy, if she recalled.

"What do you think you're doing?" she asked him.

"I'm supposed to take your temperature."

"Not with that, you're not."

"Why?"

She looked again and realised that it wasn't a needle but a thermometer. Her frazzled mind was playing tricks on her.

"Just do it then," she said to hide her embarrassment. "And next time try not to sneak up on people."

She glanced at the door, but no one had come to see what all the fuss was about. Not a single member of staff came to investigate. It was disconcerting. What if she'd been stabbed or something? Would they let her bleed to death?

ALL WAS quiet again after the nurse left. It was getting lighter now, and easier to stay awake. A little later, she heard the rattle of the trollies that signalled that breakfast was coming.

Her gaze settled on her bedside locker. She recalled having her handbag after the accident. Had she brought it with her? She couldn't remember. It was all such a blur. She opened the locker with a slight creak. Yes, there it was! She reached for it. It was a little smoky but appeared to be other-wise intact. She unzipped it and was relieved to find her mobile phone inside.

She flipped her bag open and gazed at a picture of Nathan and Bonnie in the front pocket, and a separate one of Bob. She set them on her bedside table. Then her attention turned to her phone. Phones were frowned upon on the ward, so she held it under the covers to check her messages. There were a couple of texts from Heidi. She read them and smiled. Then she opened her emails and found a long rambling one from Zoe. She rubbed her eyes and tried to make sense of it:

Prudence,

I'm sorry about bringing Mum with me to the hospital, I'm sure she's the last person you wanted to see but she was with me when I got the phone call, and I needed someone to drive me. I knew she was bad, but I never imagined she would be the cause of your accident. I'm still not sure I can quite believe it, but if she was the one responsible, then I'm deeply sorry.

The thing is, my mum is not like other mums. I didn't understand this until I started university and got to meet new people, people like you. Mum didn't like me moving in with you, but instead of saying that, like a normal person, she put ideas in my head. She said we had to test you, to make sure you were up to the job of taking care of Bonnie. She acted like if I pulled those pranks for her, then she would let me stay. But deep down, I knew that was not true.

If Bonnie had been a boy, then Mum wouldn't have given a damn about her. Mum hates boys and men. She hated my dad, though she pretended that she loved him, and she hated my brother Jason, even when he was just a kid. If Bonnie had been a boy, then she would have pressured me to put him up for adoption. She thought that was the only way. She never understood that she was the real problem.

Nathan and I just wanted to be together, and we wanted to keep our baby, whatever sex she was.

She sent me these horrible websites to look at. One was all about adoption, and another for abortion. I couldn't have gone through with either of these options, but I have to admit I thought about it because I was so desperate to get away from her. I'm convinced now that my mum killed Nathan. He was the one person who was never fooled by her for a minute. He was onto her from the start. He could tell when she was lying, and he didn't want me to be around her. He didn't want Bonnie around her either. He told me he thought she was toxic, and he said that if I kept her in my life, then she would keep on bringing me down, and then she would do the same to Bonnie. At first, I wasn't ready to accept what he was saying, but the longer I was away from her, the more confident I grew and I started to see that Nathan was right.
When Nathan was alive, I was strong enough to cut her off. I didn't need her, so long as I had him. She could see that. That's why she got rid of him. So that she could go back to controlling me, and Bonnie.

I've decided to confront her and force her to confess. I'm going to get the truth out of her if it kills me. My life doesn't matter now, but Bonnie has everything to live for, so I need you to take her because you're a better mother than I could ever be.

Horrified, Prudence dialled Zoe's number, but there was no answer.

"Come on, Zoe, pick up!"

She forwarded the message to Heidi and tried Zoe again, but there was no answer.

She slid out of bed, but her arm was still hooked up to the IV. She could call a nurse and ask her to unhook her but that would take time and she wasn't in the mood to get into a debate about it. She tugged the thin tube. She checked the door. No one was watching. She held her breath and yanked it out. The tape hurt when she pulled it, but she could take it. Good thing she was dosed up on pain meds.

She took an experimental step forward. Oh, for goodness' sake, she had a catheter in too! She pulled the curtain so the nosey woman in the next bed wouldn't see, then she leaned down and started to pull that out too. Tears smarted in her eyes and she almost reconsidered, but then she got hold of herself. *You gave birth once, remember? You can do anything.*

She gritted her teeth and eased it out. Damn, that stung. She found a small piece of gauze in her handbag to stop the bleeding. Fingers crossed that she hadn't just given herself an infection.

She staggered through the ward and out into the waiting room. Heidi had promised she would wait out here all night and Prudence had absolute faith in her. Heidi had to be here somewhere, but as she scanned the length of the corridor, her best friend was nowhere to be seen. She couldn't believe it. Heidi had promised she would stay and now, when Prudence needed her, she wasn't here.

A group of nurses stood hunched over an iPhone at reception. None of them looked up as she hobbled past. There were ripples of laughter. Apparently, whatever they were watching was highly amusing.

She made it to the door before anyone noticed her.

"Oy, where are you off to?" one of them called.

"I have to leave." There was no time for explanations.

"What, dressed like that?"

She looked down and saw that she was still in her nightdress. No matter, she'd seen people dressed worse in Morrisons.

The nurse tilted her head. Perhaps she recognised her. She hoped not. "You need to wait until the doctor comes round."

"That could be hours," Prudence said. She kept walking until she reached the lift.

The doors opened and she hopped in. She hit the button and the lift trundled slowly down to the ground floor. When the doors opened, she came face to face with Heidi. She stepped out of the lift and walked past her, towards the doors.

"Pru? Where are you going?" Heidi called after her.

Prudence turned and faced her. "You said you were going to stay here all night."

"I did! I just had to go down to the car park to pay for my parking. It had run out."

Prudence stopped. "Oh. Well, I'm afraid you've wasted your money because I need you to drive me somewhere."

"Shouldn't you be taking it easy? Where is it you want to go?"

"Zoe's house. I wouldn't ask, but I'm worried about her. She sent me a really disturbing email."

Heidi tilted her head. "Funny you should say that. I got a text from her just now. A really weird one. She told me to get the fuck out of her life."

"Show me!"

Heidi pulled out her phone and located the offending message. "It reads like the ramblings of a madwoman."

Prudence scanned it in alarm. "I don't think this is from Zoe."

35

ZOE

Zoe picked a daisy from the grass and plucked the petals one by one. Bonnie lay beside her, finally asleep after grizzling on and off all afternoon. She hadn't liked being left with their neighbour like that. Even though her mum could charm anyone, the neighbour was not a natural with children. She had tried to feed Bonnie apple sauce, and Bonnie's stomach had been rejecting it ever since. She couldn't blame the old woman, though. It wasn't her fault Zoe had no backbone. She should have stood up to her mum and insisted on bringing Bonnie with them to the hospital. They had only left her behind because Mum wanted to torture Prudence. Even a glimpse of Bonnie would have brightened up her day, and Alana wasn't prepared to give her that.

She lay back beside Bonnie and thought about what Jason had said to her on the phone.

"I hate to break it to you, but Mum's a psychopath."

For some reason, Zoe had burst out laughing.

Jason had sounded annoyed. "Think about it, Zoe. The day before Dad died, you were packed off to Gran's house, even though we all hated the old bat. Mum didn't even give you any warning, did she? She just sent you off for the week, and by the time you came back everything was dealt with. All of Dad's stuff was gone, all his clothes, all his books. It was as if he'd never existed. She filled his half of the wardrobe with all her stuff.

"I spent the week wandering the neighbourhood. Mum had me cleaning cars, mowing lawns and trimming hedges. Any way I could earn a quid or two. She told the neighbours I was saving for space camp but the sad truth was that Mum just wanted me out of the house so I wouldn't be there when the police came round. And if I earned a little money, even better. She made me hand it all over for 'safekeeping', but I wasn't daft. I kept half back. I had to bury it in a hole in the garden. How sad is that? Because I knew if I kept it anywhere in the house, Mum would find it. She had a sixth sense that way.

"People say psychopaths lack empathy, but that's not true in Mum's case. She has an incredible gift for empathy. She can tune in exactly to how other people are feeling. It's almost as if she can read their minds. She finds people fascinating. I think it's because she doesn't get the full range of human emotions herself, but boy can she manipulate! She can make instant friends with someone and make them do stuff for her, like how she used to get the neighbours to babysit for free. She is wicked at selling too. I looked her up. She's been the top estate agent at her firm for the past five years. It doesn't surprise me one bit that she's good at selling. The only thing that surprises me is that she's stuck it that long because, as you know, Mum gets bored really easily.

"You getting pregnant with Bonnie must have been exciting for her. The plot twist she'd been waiting for. That's what she's always after. She craves excitement. She's always got to have something going on. It's like a drug for her. The sad thing is, I bet her interest in Bonnie fades quickly and then she'll be chasing the next new thing."

"But what am I supposed to do about it?" Zoe had cut in. "I know what she's like but I just can't seem to break away from her. I had my own life at uni. And then I had Nathan and Bonnie, and Mum still managed to screw it up for me. I don't know what to do now. I don't know how to get away. Everything is repeating itself, over and over. I wish Dad was still here. Everything would have turned out so different."

Jason had been quiet for a moment. "It was partly my fault, about Dad."

Zoe's throat had gone dry. "What ... what do you mean?"

"Gran told me something, at Granddad's funeral."

"I don't even remember Granddad's funeral."

"You were just a little kid at the time, but Gran asked me to be one of the pall bearers. It was meant to be a big honour. I was so proud to be chosen but I realised later that no one else wanted to do it. Mum didn't even want to go to the funeral. Gran made her. She made her do a lot of things ..."

He had fallen silent again, and Zoe had waited. She could tell there was more to come.

"Afterwards, everyone was drinking. Gran let me have a beer, even though I was way too young. She had a sherry herself. It was the only time I've ever seen her drink. She didn't look like she was enjoying it. She slammed back the glass and gave a little shudder. Then she turned to me and said: 'I've got something to tell you, Jason.'

"Mum had already taken you home. She couldn't stand to be there a moment longer than she had to and you were little so she could use you as an excuse. I think she made up some nonsense about it being your bedtime or something, like either of us ever had one of those. So Gran took me outside and we sat on the steps while she smoked a cigarette and then she looked at me with a straight face and said: 'If I had my way, you'd never have been born, Jay.'

Zoe had exploded. "Oh my god, what a bitch!"

"I was too shocked to react. I just looked at her and said, 'What do you mean?' and she pulled that funny face of hers, like something smelled bad, and ever so quickly she said, 'The man you call Dad is not your dad. He's just Zoe's dad'."

Zoe dropped the phone and when she found it again, Jason had gone.

"Shit!" she'd screamed. "For god's sake, come back!"

There were long agonised minutes while she waited for him to call her back. She couldn't believe she'd got cut off during such an important conversation. She desperately wanted to hear the rest, but she feared she already knew. She wiped her sweaty palms on her shorts and checked the phone again. *For god's sake! Call, Jason.*

The phone had finally rung.

"I'm sorry," she'd apologised. "I dropped the phone. I just—"

"I know."

They'd both fallen silent, suddenly shy.

"Zoe, before I tell you this, I need to know it doesn't change anything. We are still family. Our parents don't define us. We are still who we are and ..."

"Just tell me, Jason. I need to know."

She'd heard him breathing down the line and pictured him, scratching the back of his neck the way he used to when he was nervous. Did he still have the same unruly hair or was he balding now?

"Gran wouldn't tell me anymore, but I put two and two together. I know Mum married Dad in a hurry, and it had nothing to do with love. Not on her part, anyway. Dad loved her, I'm sure of that. He was always looking at her with that lovesick expression, like he couldn't believe his luck. I always thought it was weird because no one else's parents behaved like that. Back when I used to go to school, half the kids' parents hated each other and the ones that were together had this jaded look about them, like they were just going through the motions. But Dad really did love Mum. He was always doing stuff for her, like bringing her flowers and other little gifts. I used to think it was romantic, but then I realised he was shit-scared of losing her, because he never thought he was good enough for her. That's why he let her treat him so bad. And I think that's why he went along with all her bullshit. He didn't dare stand up to her because he thought if he did, it would be over, and he was right, just not in the way he thought.

"The thing is, even Dad thought he was my dad. Mum tricked him. She made him think he'd got her pregnant. They got married within months of meeting. He was an honourable man. He had no idea there was anyone else."

"But who—"

"I think Grandad was my dad."

Zoe had retched. She'd wanted to object, but she'd felt a little tingle down her spine as she'd pictured her grandfather, running his long bony fingers through his unkempt hair.

"I never liked him," she'd stated. "I just didn't know why."

"You remember the way they used to look at each other over Sunday dinner? Mum would glare at him, and he would just sort of smirk. He was always really nice to us, but even then I could tell something was off. The house vibrated with anger whenever he was around. No one ever argued, they all said the right words to each other, played at happy families, but it all felt too polite, too staged. Like any minute the director was going to yell 'cut'.

"So one day, about a year after Granddad's funeral, I finally got up the courage and asked Mum point blank if Granddad was my dad."

"What did she say?"

"At first, she acted like she hadn't heard, so I asked her again, this time a bit louder. She shook her head and called me a disgusting little boy. I hoped I'd got it wrong. Then I said, 'But who is my dad?'

"And she just yelled at me to get out. That was the day she sent you away. The day before ..."

He was crying now, sobbing down the phone.

"I always thought Dad killed himself because he found out the truth, but then Prudence told me about Nathan. Now I think Mum killed Dad pre-emptively, so that I couldn't tell him. I don't know why she killed him and not me. I'd like to think it's because I'm her son and she loved me, but we both know that isn't true."

Zoe had gulped for air. "Maybe she was just tired of lying to him. By killing him, she was finally setting him free."

"Setting herself free, more like."

"So where did you go, after you left us? Mum said you'd run away to London. She said you'd become a rent boy and you were hooked on drugs."

Jason had snorted. "Nice future she pictured for me. I actually went and stayed with Gran for about six months. I hated her too, but I didn't have enough money to get a place on my own. I needed somewhere to stay while I saved up. I asked Gran not to tell her. I knew if she was good for one thing, it was keeping secrets."

Zoe had exhaled. "Our family is so messed up. I feel like we're trapped in a bloody hamster wheel. It just goes on and on."

"That's why you've got to stop it, Zoe. For your daughter's sake. You've got to stop the cycle."

Bonnie had started to stir, and Zoe had reluctantly let Jason go. She realised now that her whole life and everything in it had been a lie, and that included her dad. She had tried to shut out Jason and Prudence's words, but the truth was becoming impossible to ignore.

Her phone beeped and a new message from < > flashed on the screen:

"I'm worried about you. Prudence could have died. If you're ever going to leave home, now's the time."

Zoe stared at the message. How did Jason know about that? Then she checked the number and saw that it wasn't from Jason at all.

Her eyes filled with tears. She had thought no one cared about her anymore, but Prudence cared and Jason cared. And now this. If only she could find the strength to ask for help.

Z oe shot around the house, stuffing the dishes into the dishwasher and repositioning the cushions the way her mum liked them. Then she took Bonnie out of her comfy Babygro and dressed her in a flouncy sundress with big purple flowers all over it.

She heard her mum's car in the driveway. It was a new blue Lexus. Mum was smiling to herself as she walked up the path. It was an odd thing to see because her mum rarely smiled unless there was someone around to see. Perhaps she thought the neighbours might be watching.

There was a jingle of keys and then her mum was in the kitchen, straight to the fridge. Zoe heard the glug of wine being poured, then she entered the lounge, glass in hand. Her eyes flicked around the room, assessing everything from the neat little vase of posies on the mantelpiece to the scatter cushions on the sofa.

"What are we having for dinner?"

"I've ordered Thai," Zoe said. "It's on its way."

"Good." Her mother sat down beside Zoe on the sofa, her eyes on Bonnie. "How's my little Bon Bon?"

"She's fine. Mum, do you want a hold?"

"No, that's okay. I don't want to get baby goo down my new silk blouse. Tell me, Zoe. Where is Bonnie's passport?"

All at once, the room felt very cold. Zoe forced herself to meet her mother's eyes. "Bonnie doesn't have a passport."

Alana took a sip of her wine. "Is that right? Then why did you take those passport pictures of her? I found them in your wallet."

"You went through my wallet?"

"I'm only looking out for you, sweetheart. I was just wondering, though. How are you planning to get to the airport now? I mean, Nathan was supposed to drive you, wasn't he? You were all going to go together. That was the plan."

Zoe squeezed her eyes shut.

"We were going to take a little holiday. Kind of like a babymoon. To celebrate Bonnie's birth."

"Where were you planning to go?"

"I don't know. Nathan was arranging it."

Alana shook her head. "You're a terrible liar, Zoe. Now get me the tickets."

ZOE ROSE from her chair and walked upstairs to her room. She looked around in a panic. She moved things around and rustled papers. Alana appeared in the doorway.

"Where are they? I bet you have a text confirmation, don't you? Give me your phone."

Zoe reached into her pocket and handed it over. She felt useless, defeated. What did it matter now anyway? She didn't have the strength to go without Nathan.

Alana scrolled through Zoe's texts. "Taupo Airport. Where the hell's that?"

Zoe looked down at her feet. Her mum was googling. Any

minute she would—

Alana looked at her in shock. "New Zealand! You were going to run off to the other side of the world?"

"It was just a holiday," Zoe said weakly.

Alana's eyes flashed with anger. "Then why are the tickets one way?"

THE PHONE BEEPED. Another message. Zoe desperately wanted to grab it back, but Alana was looking at it curiously.

"Who's this, Zoe?"

"Just a friend."

"You don't have any friends."

"What are you typing?"

"There, that ought to do it."

She watched in horror as her mum hit 'send'. Whatever she'd written, she knew it wasn't very nice. But she couldn't react because then Alana would hang on to her phone. And she needed it. That phone was her lifeline.

THE DOORBELL SOUNDED.

"That will be the Thai food," Zoe said.

"It had better be."

Zoe trudged downstairs to the door and opened it. The driver handed her the bag.

"Enjoy your food."

"Thanks."

She dumped the bag down on the table and started pulling out plastic containers of curry and rice while her mum poured herself more wine.

"Can I have a glass?" Zoe asked.

Alana raised an eyebrow. It wasn't every day Zoe joined in with her drinking. She looked pleased. Zoe took the opportunity to slip her phone back into her pocket. She ate her dinner in silence. Thai green curry was her favourite, but she barely tasted a bite. Alana talked enough for the both of them, telling amusing anecdotes about her work. She went on about how she'd sold five houses in one day, and how she'd convinced a gormless old couple to buy a huge house they hadn't really needed, and how she was going to spend the massive commission. Zoe pretended to be impressed but she'd heard it all before, or at least variations of the same stories. She didn't mention New Zealand again, but Zoe knew that she was in trouble. She just didn't know how much.

Once she'd had enough to eat, Alana pushed her plate away and switched back to her glass.

"Now, how's work going on my new cryptocurrency? I know you've been busy with Bonnie but it's time you got back to work."

"It's going well," Zoe said. "I just need to do a bit more research."

"Right, well, when's the launch?"

"I was thinking next month."

Alana tilted her head. "I was thinking Monday."

Zoe set down her fork. "I really don't think I can have it done that quickly. You haven't even decided what you want to call it."

"That's easy: AlanaCoin."

"But last week you wanted to call it AToken."

"No, I think it should have my name in it. I'm staking my whole reputation on this, after all."

"Do you really think anyone's going to invest in it, Mum?"

"Of course, they will. I can sell anything, remember?"

"You're not going to flog it to the neighbours, are you?"

"I said everyone." She smiled a big, satisfied smile and finished her wine. Then she rose from the table and went to get more. She returned, carrying a bottle of cognac.

"Where did this come from?"

"Oh, I don't know. I popped out to the shop earlier and it was on the doorstep when I got home."

"Really?"

Alana turned the bottle over in her hands. "It looks expensive."

"Could it be from a client?" Zoe asked.

"Or an admirer," Alana said, looking pleased. She unscrewed the cap and took a sniff. "Beautiful." She poured two glasses and slid one across the table to Zoe.

"Cheers," Zoe said.

Alana clinked her glass and took a long swallow.

"I'd better put Bonnie to bed," Zoe said.

"We haven't finished discussing the AlanaCoin," her mum said.

"We will, once I've settled her down. Just give me ten minutes."

She carried her glass into the kitchen and switched on the bottle machine. Then she checked to make sure her mum wasn't watching before pouring her drink down the sink.

BONNIE TOOK HER BOTTLE QUICKLY. Her skin felt a little clammy. She could have done with a bath, but Zoe needed to get back to her mum.

"Sorry, not tonight," she whispered.

She changed Bonnie into a more comfortable outfit and laid her down in her crib. Soon she was fast asleep, hands balled up either side of her face. Zoe gazed down at her for a moment. She looked so sweet when she was asleep.

Zoe hurried back down the stairs and collected her glass from the kitchen, then placed it on the coffee table. Alana instantly topped up Zoe's glass and her own. Zoe obliged her with a sip.

"You know, we could still use those tickets."

"We can't," Zoe said, horrified. "Nathan's is in his name. You can't change it."

"I think I could spring for one extra ticket," Alana said. "I assume you had accommodation worked out?"

"We were going to live at the university," Zoe admitted. "Nathan was going to finish his degree, and I was going to work part time."

Alana snorted. "What? You were going to give up your career for a man? He wasn't even as clever as you, Zoe. He barely even scraped onto his course. Prudence told me. I can't believe you even considered this ... this nonsense. You'd have washed your whole life down the plug hole. Now, you and I, that would be different. I could get a job at any estate agent in the country. Or I could do something completely different. I've been thinking lately that maybe I should diversify and sell used cars. It always looked like so much fun. And then there's the AlanaCoin. Once that takes off, neither of us will have to work at all."

"We don't have the right papers, Mum," Zoe said faintly. "They would have let us in as students, but you and me, that would be a bit more complicated."

"Okay, well, you can be a student then. Hell, I could be a student too. That would be fun. People are always saying we look like sisters."

Zoe set down her glass. "Mum, I really don't think this is going to work. You haven't thought this through. The flight is first thing in the morning and Bonnie and I don't even have our passports yet."

"Oh, yes you do!"

Her mum delved into her handbag and came up with two new passports.

Zoe stared. "Where did you get those?"

"Prudence had them lying about the house."

"You ... you stole them from her house?"

Alana laughed. "It's hardly stealing! They're mine!"

"Mine," Zoe corrected, but she knew her mum didn't care.

They drank in silence. Zoe thought the cognac looked a little cloudy, but Alana didn't seem to notice.

"I can't keep up," she protested, as her mum filled her glass again.

"You always were a lightweight. You and lover boy had that in common."

Zoe sucked in a breath and forced herself to relax. "Still, it's nice to be able to have a drink without someone stuffing a coaster under my glass," she said with a wry smile.

Alana looked amused. "Did she really do that?"

"She did. She couldn't bear to get anything on her precious coffee table."

Alana leaned back. "It must have been so stifling, living under her roof."

Zoe forced out a laugh. "Did I tell you about her collection of china elephants? Totally tragic."

"I wonder what she'll do now?" Alana mused. "Rattling round that dump by herself, not even a dog to keep her company."

"It was a shame about the dog," Zoe said. "I thought someone would nick him. It didn't occur to me he'd get run over."

"Yes, someone must have been driving quite fast."

Zoe stiffened. *Was that an admission?* "I'm not sure I'm ever going to learn to drive," she said. "Nothing good ever comes of it. Look at poor Nathan."

She reached over and refilled her mum's glass again.

Alana took a thoughtful sip. "I don't think driving was Nathan's problem. He couldn't handle his booze, poor love. One drink and he was anyone's."

Zoe gasped. She didn't mean to; it was an involuntary reaction.

Alana looked at her, amused.

"Oh, sorry, darling, you didn't need to know that. But seriously, he thought he could take you away from me. He had it all figured out. He even threatened me with an injunction. As if a stupid piece of paper could keep me from the people I love."

Zoe could barely breathe. The room was going fuzzy. This was how she had felt, the day Nathan had died. A shrill sound built in her ears, getting louder until she could no longer hear what her mum was saying. She saw spots in front of her eyes and felt her cheeks burn. She pressed her fingers into her ears. She couldn't pass out now. She had to make it stop. With a shaking hand, she brought her remaining cognac to her lips and swallowed it down. She reached for the bottle.

"We need more cognac," she said flatly.

"There's plenty of wine in the fridge."

"But I want something stronger."

Alana nodded and knocked hers back, then picked up her car keys. Drink-driving had never been a concern for her; after all, she was convinced she was immune to alcohol.

"You'd better stay with Bonnie," she said, as she headed towards the garage.

"Bonnie's asleep," Zoe said, with a calmness she didn't feel. "She'll be fine."

Alana seemed to consider this for a moment, but she didn't object.

THE LIGHTS FLICKERED in the garage as they approached the Lexus.

"What do you think of my new wheels?" Alana asked.

"Very nice. What happened to the old car?"

"It got stolen. It's okay, though, the insurance company will pay out. I'll make sure of that."

They got into the car and Zoe fiddled with her seatbelt. Alana didn't bother with hers. She never did on a short drive. She started the car.

"Mum, wait! Do you think Bonnie will be alright? Growing up without a dad."

Alana snorted. "What do you think she needs a dad for? Anyway, you did alright."

"I missed him," she said. "I still do."

Alana looked aghast, as if this possibility had never crossed her mind.

"Why?" she asked. "He was thick as pig shit. He couldn't even earn above the minimum wage."

"He was my dad."

Alana seemed to consider this for a moment. "I don't miss my dad. In fact, I make a point of pissing on his grave every time I'm in the neighbourhood. We don't need men for anything, Zoe. They're only good for one thing – fathering children."

Zoe looked at her with fascination. She was definitely slurring her words. Alana yawned widely. Zoe yawned too. She needed to keep her talking, but she could barely keep her own eyes open. Her saliva had a bitter taste to it. Probably because she'd crushed all her antidepressants up and stirred them into the bottle of cognac. She folded her arms across her body and let her head lull to one side.

Alana's lips twitched. "Hmm, you know what I think?"

Zoe shook her head. Cold fear clutched at her heart. She could detect a bitter aftertaste. She'd hoped it wouldn't be noticeable, but her mother was looking at her with a distinctly suspicious air. If she so much as suspected, Zoe was screwed.

37

PRUDENCE

Prudence glanced at the speedometer. "Can we go a bit faster?" she asked. "I still can't get Zoe or Alana on the phone and I'm worried."

"Maybe they've gone out," Heidi suggested. Her eyes shone as she stepped on the accelerator. She wasn't in the habit of exceeding the speed limit and she seemed to find it exhilarating.

"What I don't understand is why Nathan didn't confide in me. It seems like he and Zoe were going through hell trying to get away from Alana, but he never so much as hinted to me about what the problem was, even after Bob died. I thought we were close, but I had no idea what was going on in his life those last few months."

"I think he was trying to prove how grown up and independent he was," Heidi said, changing lanes. "He wanted to prove he could stand on his own two feet and take care of his family, not go running to his mum at the first sign of trouble. It's totally understandable."

Prudence fell silent.

"Are you alright?" Heidi asked.

"I think I'm going to be sick."

"Do you want me to get off at the next junction?"

"No, I just need a bag or something."

"There's a grocery bag on the back seat. Just empty out the onions." Heidi checked the satnav. "It's not far now. I think ..."

She glanced in the mirror and Prudence followed her gaze. A fleet of blue lights was fast approaching, but there was nowhere to pull over.

"I'm going to get off here," Heidi decided. She prodded the satnav, programming in a new route to Alana's house.

Prudence held the grocery bag on her lap and watched as the police finally manoeuvred past the traffic. There were three police cars and an ambulance, too, all in rapid succession. She leaned over the bag, but the smell of onions made her feel worse, so she wound down the window.

"Nearly there," Heidi said.

They turned onto a smaller road. There was nothing but fields for a couple of miles, but then they reached the village.

"I recognise the pub on the corner," she told Heidi. "You need to slow down or you'll miss the turning."

Heidi stamped on the brakes, causing the driver behind them to honk his horn. "Sorry!" She took a sharp right and turned into Russet Way.

THERE WERE EMERGENCY VEHICLES EVERYWHERE. An ambulance was parked on the grass in the middle of the cul-de-sac and police tape hung across the driveway. Prudence's heart beat faster, as she took in the scene.

They ditched the car in front of a neighbour's house. They were blocking the driveway but Prudence didn't care. She had to get to her girls. She had to know if they were alright.

Her legs felt like lead as she staggered towards the house. Heidi strode ahead of her, not seeming to notice her struggle.

Zoe's last words floated back to her: 'I've decided to confront her and force her to confess. I'm going to get the truth out of her if it kills me.'

Zoe, what have you done?

HEIDI REACHED one of the police officers and tapped him on the shoulder. Prudence strained to hear their conversation. To her great frustration, she couldn't hear a thing. Heidi turned and waved at her to hurry up, but she was already going as fast as she could.

"I'm afraid there's been a serious incident," the police officer said when she finally reached him.

Prudence clenched her stomach. "What? What's happened?"

"Who are you exactly?"

"She's the grandmother," Heidi said for her.

"Right, well, in that case I'm going to have to ask you to wait a few minutes. This is a terribly sad situation and ..."

Prudence's jaw dropped as an ambulance crew emerged from the garage, dressed in masks and breathing apparatus.

"Oh god, it's carbon monoxide poisoning, isn't it?" Everything went blurry. Blue lights danced before her eyes. She felt a burst of pain in her heart and knew that whatever it was, she couldn't take it. *If anything had happened to Bonnie, she would die.*

"Please," Heidi begged. "Just put her out of her misery! Tell us what's going on."

The police officer cleared his throat. "I'm afraid there has been a fatality."

"Oh god."

"Look!" Heidi pointed as the door to the house opened and Zoe emerged.

"Zoe!" Prudence yelled, her voice too hoarse to make much sound. "Zoe, I'm here, love!"

Zoe looked up. Her eyes were bloodshot, her face was white. One of the police officers had a guiding hand on her arm. She was walking oddly, with both hands behind her back. It was only then that Prudence realised she had been handcuffed.

"I'm so sorry," she mouthed.

"Zoe! Where's Bonnie?"

Zoe shook her head, too overwhelmed to speak.

Prudence's voice grew louder. "Where is she?"

Then a policewoman stepped out of the house, carrying a struggling baby.

"Bonnie! I'm her grandmother! Give her to me!" Prudence felt as though a huge weight had lifted from her shoulders. She stepped towards her granddaughter and spoke with the police officer, who demanded to see some identification before she would let her anywhere near Bonnie.

"Prudence ..."

She turned and looked questioningly at Heidi.

"What is it?"

"They've taken Zoe away."

"You know what I think?" Alana said.

"What?" Zoe reluctantly replied. She held a finger over her seatbelt, ready to release.

"I think I'd better take that phone of yours, just for safe-keeping."

Alana held out her hand and Zoe pulled her phone from her pocket. Her hand shook as she placed it in her mother's hand.

"Who was that texting you, anyway? You never said."

Zoe scoured her mind for an explanation. Whatever answer she gave, she knew it would be wrong.

"It was just Heidi. She's a friend of Prudence's. I think the old prune told her what a crap mum I am and now she wants to take me under her wing."

Alana smirked. "Not after the reply I sent her. I doubt she'll ever bother you again. But just in case, let me handle her. If she thinks she can come between me and my daughter, she's got another thing coming."

"Mum, wait. About Nathan. Did he really do what you said?"

Alana's face twisted silently. "He would have, sweetheart. Believe me, men are all the same."

"But they don't have to be," she argued. "Nathan was different. I really think he would have been a brilliant dad."

Alana gave a big yawn and closed her eyes, as if Nathan wasn't worth a second thought.

"He called me and asked me to meet him, not at home, sweetheart, but somewhere private. He suggested a bar."

Alana was watching her as she said this. She seemed to enjoy the hurt in Zoe's eyes.

"I only went because I was curious what he wanted. He didn't strike me as the forward type, but you never know with men. Like I've told you before, they're all fatally flawed. He was just finishing work when I arrived. He was wearing that dreadful uniform. I couldn't be seen out in public with him like that, so I made him take off the jacket. Luckily, he was wearing a T-shirt underneath."

Zoe bit her lip. How could her mother go on about what Nathan was wearing? How did that even matter in the great scheme of things? But these little things mattered very much to Alana. They always had.

"When we got to the bar, Nathan wanted to order a Coke, but I told him he could have it with whiskey, like a man. That place was a dive. All the tables were sticky and the music was just dreadful. We could barely hear ourselves speak. Anyway, he told me what he was planning. He was going to take out an injunction, to keep me away from you and Bonnie. He thought it was only fair to give me a warning. He said it was a shame because a child really needed grandparents, but that in my case he felt he was acting in his family's best interests. I listened to him politely. I told him that I was shocked because I only wanted the best for my family, and I asked if there was anything I could do to change his mind. He seemed placated by that and said that if I kept away for a while, then the pair of you would consider letting me back in Bonnie's life. I think he mentioned supervised visits, or something equally inadequate. I pretended to cling to that idea. I said I'd do anything to be allowed back into Bonnie's life, and I wasn't lying.

"We drank to the future and I wished him well. He couldn't hold his drink, poor boy, so by the time the bar closed he was a bit wobbly. The barman noticed and handed me his keys. I said not to worry because I would take care of him. And I did."

Bile rose in Zoe's throat and she swallowed. "How did he get home, if you took his keys?"

"I drove him, of course. I had drunk just as much as he had, but the alcohol didn't affect me. I was just fine to drive. It's a good thing it was late because I wouldn't have been seen dead driving that old heap of junk, but no one was around to see us. When we arrived at the Prune's house, I tucked the car into the garage. Nathan was really sleepy by then but I persuaded him he would be more comfortable on the back seat. After all, if he went inside now, he might wake Bonnie.

"He didn't even question it, the silly boy. He seemed only too happy to climb into the back and lay down his head. A part of me even wonders if he knew what I was doing. It must have been difficult for him, working such long hours. So much pressure to keep his family afloat. Wouldn't it be so much easier just to go to sleep for a while? Anyway, that's where I left him, sleeping like a baby.

"I left the engine running. It can get awfully cold outside at night, and I opened a couple of windows for ventilation. Then I slipped out into the night. I'd parked my car in a little road behind the station. It was a long journey, but I had sobered up nicely from the drive. I popped home and took a shower to freshen up and then I was the first one in the office as always. No one even knew I'd been gone."

Zoe let out a puff of air and rested her head against the

car seat. Hearing those words was painful. She had hoped so badly that her mum would have another explanation. She had wanted so much to be wrong.

She looked at her mother now and assessed her condition. Alcohol never affected her very much, but she had drunk more than usual tonight. And the pills – it looked like they were having some effect. Alana should have started to drive, but instead she slumped forwards, over the steering wheel, and there she lay, too exhausted to move.

As Zoe watched, a feeling of total calmness swept over her. The gentle purr of the engine reminded her of a neighbour's cat. She felt warm, like she was lying in the sun. Sunbathing on a perfect white beach, the waves lapping in and out in a gentle rhythm.

The waves were getting louder, crashing against the rocks. Zoe tried to ignore them, but there were gulls circling overhead, flapping, shrieking.

"Waa! Waa!"

Not gulls. Bonnie. Bonnie was crying.

Reluctantly, she opened one eye. Yes, definitely Bonnie. Where was she?

She sat up. Alana was still draped over the steering wheel. Her back rose and fell with each breath. Zoe reached for the door handle and softly opened the car door. She turned her body, ready to step down from the car when a hand clutched at her sleeve.

"Don't leave me!" her mum murmured.

Zoe couldn't even tell if she was awake.

"I'll be right back," she whispered, but the hand became a vice around Zoe's wrist.

Her heart pounded in her chest. Why couldn't her mother just let her go?

Bonnie was still crying, her shrieks growing louder the

longer they went unanswered. Then she fell silent, and Zoe was even more frightened.

She peeled her mother's fingers off, one by one. The nails were long and jagged, and she was wearing an icy blue nail polish that looked eerie in the dim light. Gently as she could, Zoe extricated herself from her mother's grip and then she took one last look at the woman she had spent most of her life with.

Slowly, she slipped out of the car and shut the door softly behind her. She tiptoed through the garage and stood in the doorway for a moment, waiting to see if her mum would follow, but she continued to lie there, eyes closed, as Zoe found the door handle and let herself out of the garage.

Bonnie was howling again as Zoe hurried up the stairs. She must have been taking a breather, because now her howls echoed around the house as she vented all her fury. Zoe paused to catch her breath on the landing, then stepped into her daughter's perfect pink nursery.

"It's okay, darling. Mummy's coming,"

Bonnie had somehow rolled onto her front and was crying indignantly, demanding to be rolled back to her preferred position. Zoe lifted her out of the cot and held her tight, gazing down at her large blue eyes, so like Nathan's. She carried her over to the window and opened it so she could breathe in the fresh night air. She could still feel the effects of the cognac. Bonnie was probably due for a feed, and she'd better make herself some strong coffee while she was at it.

She kissed the top of Bonnie's head.

"I thought I couldn't be a mum, but I was wrong. You saved me with all your crying, and my mother's instinct woke me up. I might not be the best mum in the world, but I can't be any worse than my mum. And you've got your daddy watching over you. He will be there always. We're going to be alright now, Bonnie. I promise you."

EPILOGUE
PRUDENCE

"It's just like visiting the airport," Prudence told Bonnie, mainly for the benefit of the little girl behind them, who was looking nervously at the machine they used to scan their possessions. She would have preferred not to bring a bag with her on these visits, but she had to bring some milk and other supplies for Bonnie.

She loaded everything onto the tray and then waited while she and Bonnie were patted down. Was it really necessary to manhandle a baby like that?

"You'd be surprised what people smuggle into nappies," the prison guard snapped, catching her look.

He thrust Bonnie back into her arms.

"Go ahead."

Bonnie gave him a little wave, but he looked right through her. Prudence placed her bag in a locker and carried Bonnie through to the visitor's room. The atmosphere was gloomy and soulless, despite the pile of children's toys in the corner. Prudence tried to imagine that they were meeting Zoe at a café, perhaps her favourite one in the park. Poor Zoe, she couldn't imagine being cooped up all day and rarely allowed out into the fresh air. Prudence didn't know how she stood it.

Acid burned in her stomach as she clamped eyes on Zoe. She'd had her hair cut extremely short. The cut was much too severe for her face. It made her look older and tougher. Perhaps that was the point. Or maybe it was just easier to take care of.

It was painful to see her this way. Just recently, she'd been looking through some photos from her retirement party. Zoe's skin had been almost luminous then, cheeks flushed, eyes shining brightly. Now she was just a shell of the woman her son had fallen in love with.

She sat down opposite Zoe at one of the stark metal tables. Bonnie was already squirming in her arms, but Prudence was determined to keep her on her lap. She didn't like the thought of her playing on the dirty linoleum floor, and she didn't like the look of the toys either. She wondered if anyone ever washed them between visits.

"Thank you for coming," Zoe said.

"Of course, we came," Prudence said. "Bonnie wanted to see her mummy."

"I mean, I know it's a long way ..."

"It doesn't matter how far you are, we'll always come," Prudence told her firmly. Zoe's eyes glistened and Prudence touched her hand and tried to block out the prison guards, stationed either side of the room. It was so hard to be natural when you knew you were being watched.

Zoe ran a hand through what was left of her hair.

"Was there much traffic?" she asked.

"Oh, you don't want to hear about that!" Prudence said. "I want to know how you're getting on. Are they treating you okay? Do you need anything?"

"I'm fine," Zoe said. "I think the other inmates are scared of me. Because of what I did."

Prudence cast an eye at the watchers.

"Be careful what you say," she warned.

"Because of them? I don't care. I did what I did. I'm not going to deny it."

Prudence pressed her lips together. "You've got a good lawyer. But the fact is, you could be here a while. The good news is that they're confident they can get you a place in the mother and baby unit. Isn't that wonderful? You'll be able to have Bonnie in with you."

She had hoped Zoe would be cheered at this news, but her face became even more set than before.

"No, I could never do that to Bonnie. She hasn't done anything. Why should she be put in jail? She's far better off on the outside, with you."

Prudence clutched Bonnie tighter. "But you hardly get to see her, Zoe. And the mother and baby unit is nicer, on account of the children. I'm sure you'd have an easier time of it in there. You must be missing her?"

"I do miss her. Every day. But I know she's in safe hands with you."

Prudence looked deep into Zoe's eyes and she met her gaze, blankly.

"You're being very brave," she told her, swallowing the lump in her throat.

Zoe gave a careless shrug, but Prudence caught the way her eyes flicked towards the prison officer and then the door.

"Are you sure there's nothing you need? I've sent you a postal order, but if there's anything else, just let me know."

"I would like some more pictures of Nathan and Bonnie. I managed to spill coffee over the ones I had. Could you print some more out for me?"

"Of course. I could get them laminated. That way they'll be easier to keep clean."

"That would be great, thanks."

Prudence leaned forward. "How are you getting along with the other inmates? Have you made any friends?"

"They're all messed up," Zoe said sadly. "Every single one of them. Some of them have had their kids taken off them and put in care. It's so sad. And there are a lot of fights. People seem to lose it over the slightest thing. But don't worry about me. I'm keeping my head down."

"What about your cellmate? What's she like?"

"Old. She's been around a while. She's looking out for me."

"That's nice."

Zoe's eyes swept the room again, not lingering too long on any one person.

"Do you ever dream about Nathan?" she asked suddenly.

"I haven't for a while," Prudence said. "Have you?"

Zoe nodded. "I dreamt we were all together again. It felt so real that I almost believed that he was still with me. He was asking me what I wanted for breakfast, and I said I'd have whatever he was having, but he said, 'No, Zoe. You've got to make your own choice.' He was always like that. You know, with my mum, every choice was a trap. But Nathan taught me that there wasn't a right or wrong answer to every question, there was just his opinion and my opinion, and if they were different then we could talk about it. He was the most amazing person I ever met and I will hold him in my heart forever."

"As will I," Prudence said. "We have to be strong for him, Zoe. I know he would hate to see you in a place like this. But you're going to get out one day. I know you're doing everything you can to rebuild your life for this little one."

"Can I ... can I hold her?"

"Of course, you can."

As Zoe opened her arms, Prudence couldn't help but notice the bruises on her wrist. Biting back the question on her lips, she passed Bonnie across the table. Bonnie gave a little wail of protest, then to her relief she settled in her mother's arms.

"Have you spoken to Jason since you've been here?"

Zoe nodded. "He wrote to me and asked if it would be okay if he came to visit."

"Have you written back?"

"Not yet, but I'm going to. I just don't quite know where to begin. I don't know why he's bothering with me, given the way I treated him before."

"I tell you what, if you can ask for some paper and a pen I could help you write that letter?"

Zoe smiled. "Thank you. I'd like that."

She looked down at Bonnie, taking a moment to study her face.

"Mum assumed that if Bonnie had been a boy I'd get rid of him. I was appalled at first, but then I wondered if it might be for the best to give the baby away. But since Bonnie was a girl, I needed to get her away from Mum, to stop her controlling her life, the way she's controlled mine."

"But you had me and Nathan ..."

Zoe nodded. "It took me a while to realise that you are not like my mum. And then, once Bonnie was born, I finally saw it. And I saw how great Nathan was with her too. I really thought everything was going to be okay because me and Nathan, we had a plan you see. We were going to take out an injunction against her. Nathan really thought it would work. We knew Mum wouldn't like it but I never thought she would go so far as to stop us. The trouble is, Nathan had such a good heart. He found it hard to believe the worst about people. I think he wanted to make her understand. He never told me he was meeting her, the night he died. But I think he just wanted to talk to her, to give her one last chance. Because he always wanted to do the right thing. If only he'd told me, I would have stopped him. But he didn't and now he's dead."

A tear dripped on to the table and Zoe hurriedly wiped her eyes. "I'd never have let him go alone."

Prudence drew a breath. "Did you really think it would work, this injunction?"

"Nathan did, but I was more pessimistic. That's why we had a back-up plan. We were planning a whole new life in New Zealand, just me, Nathan and Bonnie."

"So that's why you had that brochure in your room?"

"I thought if Mum wouldn't leave us alone, then we'd go somewhere she would never find us. We had it all arranged. We were just waiting for the passports to come through. Heidi helped with that. I told her we wanted to take a little holiday and I got her to countersign the forms because I needed someone who could verify who we both were. She signed it, even though she hadn't known me long enough. She lied for me as a favour to Nathan."

"She never said."

"Well, I think she got the feeling you didn't like me very much."

Zoe looked at her shyly.

Prudence shook her head. "Can't say I did at first. You're growing on me, though. I'm starting to see what Nathan saw in you. Were you ever going to tell me where you were going?"

"Of course we would have!" Zoe spoke a little too quickly.

"Hmm ..."

"I have to admit I found it hard to trust you at first, but after a while I began to feel differently about you, once I saw that you are nothing like my mum."

Prudence leaned forward. "No matter what happens, I will be here for you and Bonnie."

"Oh, Prudence! I wish you were my mum."

"From now on, I will be."

Time was almost up. Prudence leaned over to take Bonnie back from Zoe and became aware of a shadow over their table. She looked up and saw a prison guard speaking to the prisoner at the next table. At the guard's prompting, the woman rose to her feet. Prudence caught the hard look she gave Zoe before she was led from the room.

"Zoe, are you sure you're alright in here? If you need me to have a word ..."

Zoe shook her head vehemently. "I just need you to take care of Bonnie. I want her to have the best life possible, even if that means keeping her away from me."

"But, Zoe—"

"It's my choice," Zoe said firmly. "I want Bonnie to have the childhood I never had. You can give her that. I know you can."

The prison guard returned and Zoe hugged and kissed Bonnie one last time before they were yanked away. Prudence blinked back tears as she thought of Zoe being locked away in her cold, dank cell. Bonnie gurgled contentedly in her arms as she carried her out into the light. The sun glistened on the windows as they boarded the shuttle bus back to the car park. Bonnie craned to see out the window, her little nose pressed against the glass as they waited for the rest of the visitors to board the bus.

It wasn't the retirement Prudence had always dreamed of, but she couldn't imagine her life without Bonnie in it, and if she was honest with herself, she couldn't imagine it without Zoe either.

ABOUT THE AUTHOR

Lorna Dounaeva has a Masters in European Studies and used to work at the Home Office before turning to crime fiction. She lives in Godalming, Surrey with her husband, three children and a crafty cat.

Did you enjoy *The Family Trap*? Please consider leaving a review on Amazon to help other readers discover the book.

www.lornadounaeva.com

ALSO BY LORNA DOUNAEVA

The Wrong Twin

The Perfect Family

The Family Trap